Gone to her Death

by
PIERRE AUDEMARS

WALKER AND COMPANY
NEW YORK

Copyright © 1981 by Pierre Audemars

All rights reserved. No part of this book may be reproduced or transmitted in any form or by any means, electric or mechanical, including photocopying, recording, or by any information storage and retrieval system, without permission in writing from the Publisher.

All the characters and events portrayed in this story are fictitious.

First published in the United States of America in 1981 by the Walker Publishing Company, Inc.

Published simultaneously in Canada by John Wiley & Sons Canada, Limited, Rexdale, Ontario.

ISBN: 0-8027-5455-4

Library of Congress Catalog Card Number: 81-51981

Printed in the United States of America

10 9 8 7 6 5 4 3 2 1

*To Joan,
whose love, help
and understanding
made it all possible.*

One more unfortunate,
Weary of breath,
Rashly importunate,
Gone to her death.

Take her up tenderly
Lift her with care,
Fashioned so slenderly,
Young and so fair.

The Bridge of Sighs
Thomas Hood 1798–1845

ONE

In the days when M. Pinaud was approaching the peak of his long and not altogether undistinguished career, one of his most cherished ambitions, which he had shared with his wife Germaine since the day of their marriage—to own an old house in the country—was suddenly and unexpectedly fulfilled.

They had both been looking for a long period, mainly at week-ends, the only time his exacting and arduous profession allowed him as his own.

Their two daughters were now both grown-up and married. It would be nice to own a place to which they could bring their families for the week-end. Its location, therefore, could not be too far from Paris, since M. le Chef's unending and peremptory demands for personal reports were not to be ignored.

At first they concentrated on something small, and consequently modest in price, since—strangely enough—in spite of all his years of hard work, and the unremitting and devoted efforts of his chronicler, the success of his astonishing exploits had never brought him any interesting amount of wealth.

But then—suddenly, unexpectedly and considerately—Germain's uncle died, leaving her more money than any of his distant relatives had ever dreamed that he possessed.

And so, with an uncontrollable enthusiasm engendered by stupefaction, joy and happiness, they did not hesitate.

The various estate-agents with whom they had dealt, now considerably more interested and definitely more civil, were galvanized into action. Within a few months the dream house at Vervion, in the rich and rolling Normandy countryside, was theirs.

When everything had been finally signed, sealed and settled, witnessed, indexed and filed, and everyone who presented a bill had been promptly paid, the amount of money left from the will's bequest would hardly have kept M. Pinaud in cigarettes for a month, but he was not unduly worried.

He comforted himself by philosophically counting his blessings. He had obviously reached a certain age—looking back, it was unbelievable how rapidly and incomprehensibly so many years had fled—but after all, who retired or even thought of retirement when they were at the height of their fame? Certainly not him.

He could look forward to several more years of employment at a salary—which although pitiful compared with the value he gave for it—was almost certainly bound to increase shortly, to compensate for inflation. M. le Chef had influential friends in the government. It was only a question of being patient and awaiting one's turn. The claims of nearly every other state-employed body of workers had been granted. The *Sûreté* could neither be overlooked nor omitted.

For several years he had had an unwritten agreement with M. le Chef. The understanding was that he would continue to work, without any irrelevant or depressing talk about retirement, for as long as he felt so remarkably fit.

This agreement was to their mutual advantage.

M. le Chef could manage his organization with typical competence, basking meanwhile in the reflected glory of being in the unique position of employing the greatest detective of this modern age. Meanwhile M. Pinaud would have the opportunity, for a few more years at least, of being able to continue with his harmless and perhaps futile—but so wonderfully comforting—hopes and dreams that one day all these fantastic and incredible cases he had solved might well bring him fame and recognition—to say nothing of more money.

And so, with incurable optimism, he had paid surveyor's fees, since the house at Vervion was nearly six hundred years old and needed some repairs, engaged the local builder, asked for a few days' leave between two particularly difficult cases, moved most of the contents of their flat in the 14th, leaving one room furnished if ever he should have to stay in town, bought more furniture, paid for the removal and installed his wife in the house.

Germaine was left with all the builder's mess, the task of making him and his two assistants innumerable cups of coffee throughout each day, and a large old-fashioned garden full of weeds, since M. Pinaud could only come at week-ends or on the odd day that he happened to be free.

Needless to say, she was supremely happy. This was naturally contagious and probably the reason for his optimism. He had been worrying M. le Chef for months to supply him with a new car—his incredible mileage was beginning to produce its inevitable results. He was bound to get one soon. Then he could drive really fast to Vervion, which would give him more time to help her with all the jobs waiting to be done.

This, briefly, was the situation. Which made both the sudden summons to M. le Chef's office on that lovely morning in May about three months after their move, and the interview that ensued, all the more unexpected, surprising and distressing.

'Ah yes—Pinaud. I wanted to see you.'

The great man did not even look up, but continued to study, with an intent absorption, the clean sheet of notepaper, on whose surface nothing was written, which he held in his hand. This was his favourite method of collecting, organizing and marshalling his varied and complicated thoughts.

M. Pinaud waited patiently in front of the desk. He was not asked to sit down, since that magnificently furnished room on the first floor held only one chair, in which his employer was already seated.

'First of all,' the carefully modulated voice said suddenly, without any expression at all, 'Let it be clearly understood that this interview is not of my own seeking. I wanted to see you because I had to. I am only doing my duty and obeying my instructions, but I find the whole thing not only distressing, but painful. Definitely painful.'

Here he paused and looked up suddenly. M. Pinaud had been waiting in a respectful silence, since no-one ever interrupted M. le Chef while he was speaking. Now he was surprised at the concern in the deep-set and hooded eyes.

'If you would be kind enough to explain, m'sieu,' he began gently, 'So that I can—'

The rules regarding interruptions did not apply to M. le Chef.

'Explain? Of course I intend to explain. That is what I am doing now. That is why you are here. What are you on now, Pinaud?'

M. Pinaud sighed profoundly, but without the slightest sound or change of expression.

'If you remember, m'sieu,' he replied quietly and politely, 'There was the body of this young boy found in the sailor's bed behind the *Gare St. Lazare*—'

'Yes—yes—of course. I remember now. Disgusting. Revolting. Well—get it cleared up and finished by Friday—'

M. Pinaud was so astonished—since this case, in spite of its unspeakable details, had all the indications of becoming one of his major triumphs—that he completely forgot all about the sacrosanct rules of interruption.

'But that is only two days—'

M. le Chef, surprisingly, did not rebuke him. Instead he leaned back in his chair and placed the fingertips of both hands under his chin. In his thoughtful regard M. Pinaud could recognize regret, concern and even affection.

'I too,' he said quietly, 'learnt to count at school, even without the aid of a calculator. I know that Friday is in two days' time. But that is the deadline. I heard this morning. Either wind it up, or else hand it over, with your notes, to someone else. You will probably have to, anyway.'

He took a deep breath before he continued:

'Let me explain. I have got to go. My official letter of resignation has already been written. But that is only a formality—to save my pride and self-respect.

'Apparently crime to-day is getting so violent and complicated that higher authority has come to the conclusion that younger men are essential—in that only they are capable of coping with it. We both know that this is nonsense, but there is nothing that we can do. This decision applies to you too, Pinaud, in spite of your magnificent record of twenty-three cases. As you know, we are both about the same age.'

He paused and smiled wryly.

'No-one would ever think it. I sometimes feel old enough to be your father. It must be that astonishing life you lead which keeps you looking so young.'

To say that M. Pinaud's thoughts were confused and chaotic would be a masterpiece of meosis.

'But—but our agreement—' he began. 'Surely you told them—'

'I am sorry. There is no written contract. And therefore nothing that can be contested. The whole matter is now out of my hands.'

As if to give point to what he had said, M. le Chef

removed his fingertips from his chin and contemplated them gravely, almost as if seeking to reassure himself, in case of any possible doubt, that they were really still part of those same hands which had actually been deprived of the matter under discussion.

Then, before his frustrated and infuriated employee could interrupt again, he continued to speak.

'This performance is known to-day as a purge. I am given to understand that it is a common enough and even a necessary procedure in these modern times. How the generation of our fathers ever managed to develop the technology of the coal and steel age, and to establish commercial empires throughout the world without them, will always naturally remain a profound mystery to me.'

He paused, and then his tone became more brisk.

'Now then, Pinaud. Next Friday is the end of the month. At six o'clock on that day there is to be an official meeting of all the staff here, in order to introduce our new ruler and his various departmental managers. And to outline their new policy. To you and to me, Pinaud, it will not matter very much. We do not need those instructions. We shall no longer be here. But to all the others, it will be an important occasion. Every employee of the *Sûreté* will be present. The word will was underlined three times in red ink on the official directive.'

'I have not seen any directive,' M. Pinaud told him quietly.

'Of course not. How could you? You have been away and busy on your case. You will probably find one on your door-mat when you get home. I have a copy here to give you, but I thought it better and more courteous to tell you its contents and these facts in my own words.'

'Thank you, m'sieu. I appreciate that.'

With a great effort he kept his voice expressionless. M. le Chef eyed him very carefully, sighed profoundly and then continued to speak.

'So get everything cleared up by Friday. If you find that impossible, hand over your notes. You will be told to whom. Probably to one of these insufferably conceited young prigs who seem to have been joining our staff at the rate of one a month during the past year. Each one has had a personal letter from the Minister himself stating that the bearer is the son of a very dear friend and could we do our utmost and so on and so forth.

'I sent the first one back with a rude reply in a carefully sealed envelope. He would have found considerable difficulty in making coffee for fifteen people, quite apart from arresting or shooting dangerous criminals. As a result, I had the Minister on the telephone for three-quarters of an hour.

'Since then, I have kept my mouth shut. Very tightly shut. And I have not written. Even so, the powers that be obviously think it better that I should join you on Friday rather than wait until I open it again.'

He stood up and held out his hand, and once again M. Pinaud was astonished at all that he could read in those hooded and deep-set eyes.

He began to speak, and then suddenly changed his mind. If M. le Chef, who had counted that particular minister as a personal friend for so many years, had arrived at the conclusion that the only thing to do was to keep his mouth shut, then there did not seem much point in opening his.

The precisely articulated voice was suddenly soft with emotion.

'We shall not be alone here on Friday, Pinaud. This moment—the two of us alone in one room—is perhaps the right time—probably the only time—to thank you, with the utmost sincerity and admiration, for all that you have done for the *Sûreté* over the past long years. At times you have upset me, annoyed me, exasperated and infuriated me—even thwarted me—but never once have you let me down. You have every right to be as proud of yourself as I am of you.

'I understand that your chronicler, in spite of all his efforts and hard work, has never really succeeded in achieving a world-wide recognition of your formidable and celebrated exploits. That is not your fault, but his. I ought to know. Each one of your twenty-three cases is detailed in my files. Instead of formulating basic principles for criminological technology, they may well be cleared out now and shredded for pulp. Life is sometimes like that.'

He waited for a moment, as if in sympathy, but M. Pinaud could not speak. His memories were too vivid, too intense and too poignant for words.

'It only remains for me to wish you God-speed and good luck in whatever you decide to do. Have you made any plans?'

M. Pinaud shook the proferred hand strongly.

'No, m'sieu,' he replied quietly. 'No plans.'

How could one make plans—when the very foundations of his whole world so suddenly seemed to have fallen in ruins?

'Never mind. Something will turn up. If you would like me to write any letters you have only to ask.'

'Thank you, m'sieu.'

'Then that is all, Pinaud. Get that case cleared up. See you on Friday.'

The interview was over.

The meeting was held in the *grand salon* on the ground floor, with white-coated waiters serving an abundance of drink and appetizing snacks.

It was superbly organized, smoky, noisy, pitifully impersonal and—to M. Pinaud—bitter in its poignant wistfulness.

He had decided—which should be noted to his credit—not to go home to his new house during those last two days. With all the alterations being effected by one sympathetic master builder and his two assistants, together with the challenge of the garden, Germaine was like a child surrounded by new toys. He considered that it would be unfair to appear suddenly and unexpectedly to destroy her happiness with the ominous significance of his news.

She did not expect him until the week-end.

He therefore concentrated all his not inconsiderable energies into persuading the maritime paedophile to meet him at an early hour in a lonely and deserted part of the *Bois de Boulogne*, where he drew his silenced gun and indulged without preamble in some fairly spectacular near-miss shooting, threatening to continue with toes, fingers and earlobes until he obtained a signed

confession.
Two toes and one finger later this was in his pocket. He had written it out himself the night before, after confirming the appointment on the telephone with a masterly insight into the man's vanity, lust and greed.

The gun remained rock steady as he reached for the handcuffs in his hip-pocket, the threat in his eyes implacable and menacing.

Now as he stood in a corner of that noisy and crowded room, with a large glass of excellent wine in his hand, he found difficulty in keeping the tears from those same eyes, whose cold and threatening hostility had so easily broken a man's nerve in the early hours of that same morning.

So many years of dedicated toil—so many risks and dangers immediately and unreservedly accepted—so much tragedy and pain, fatigue and loneliness—were they all to end like this, with a whimper and not with a bang?

He drained his glass in one gigantic swallow. An attentive waiter stepped forward smartly and refilled it immediately. M. Pinaud thanked him politely and then looked around the room again.

M. le Chef was in a far corner, talking animatedly to someone who looked like a retired admiral, but who was actually their packer and messenger.

Henri Lasaule, their new ruler, was seated at a small table in the centre of the room. The table was piled high with files, documents and papers. He was a short and burly figure, with close-cropped black hair and an immense and pugnacious jowl, clad in a silk shirt and a very expensive suit whose shade of blue was so intense as to be almost offensive.

At intervals he would raise his voice to make some announcement, declaim a short speech or read from some document, whereupon all the people in the whole room fell utterly, respectfully and attentively silent, and all the waiters ceased from their labours of filling glasses.

In M. Pinaud's opinion these pronouncements were not only unnecessary but at far too frequent intervals. Not only did they interfere, by their very frequency, with any serious drinking, but to him they also had a ring of insincerity, as if they had been too carefully rehearsed.

He therefore began to move, soundlessly and unobtrusively, as soon as that dominant and agressive voice started, in the direction of that attentive and efficient waiter, so as not to waste any valuable drinking time once it had ended. This manoeuvre he repeated with commendable success, not once but many times.

Naturally he knew most of the occupants of the room. All the other detectives were his colleagues and good friends. The only difference between them was that they were all continuing to work while he had been ordered to retire. Not even another large glass of wine could eradicate the bitterness of that thought.

But there were also, all about him, an astonishing number of new and strange faces, belonging to eager young men in wasp-waisted suits, who talked in loud and vehement voices with a brash and irritating self-confidence that sometimes even set into motion their long, undulating and stylishly waved hair.

These must be the new recruits, he reflected, of whom M. le Chef had spoken. These were the new inheritors of the earth—only because they were young.

He called out greetings to several of his acquaintances, but took great care not to leave his corner, which gave him strategic access to that waiter who had proved himself to be such a sympathetic type. Besides, he was not in a mood for conversation. All this nonsense was making him profoundly depressed.

And then suddenly the voice rasped out again, which did not surprise him very much, but the words it uttered did—to such an extent that he found himself just too far away from his friend the waiter for that worthy to be of any help to him.

'And therefore to M'sieu Pinaud, as a token of appreciation for so many years of loyal and faithful service, we have great pleasure in presenting him with his car as a personal gift. It was considered that this would be a far more practical recognition of our gratitude, in these days of inflation, than any bonus, especially as we hear that he has just bought a house in the depths of the country.'

Somehow—he did not know how—he got rid of his glass and found himself standing beside the small table, shaking hands with Lasaule, thanking him politely and listening to all the hand-clapping as if in a dream.

He looked desperately across the room at M. le Chef, but that individual was far too busy clapping his hands to meet his eye.

How could such things be happening to him? For

nearly two years he had been pestering M. le Chef for a new car, but without success. And now they had given it to him, instead of a fat cheque with which he could have bought a new one. This one had been a very good car. This was still a good car, but now, not surprisingly, it was practically worn out.

He opened his mouth to speak, his mind already rehearsing with lightning-like rapidity a few well-chosen, tactful and apt remarks—without wishing to look a gift horse in the mouth, m'sieu, I am sure that if you could spare me a few moments in the company of M'sieu le Chef, he will surely confirm that this car—when he became aware that the other voice was speaking instead of his own.

'And here is the detail of your pension from the Records Office.'

He took the proferred document and read the figures swiftly and with a great and stupefied dismay. This was chicken-feed. In these days on inflation it was a bad joke. Each quarterly cheque would about enable him to buy two new tyres for his car.

He made a great effort to keep calm. He spoke quietly, just to the man at the table.

'Thank you, m'sieu. But may I say that I find the amount here—in view of the very high contributions I have always made from my salary over the years—'

'Yes—yes, M'sieu Pinaud,' the aggressive voice interrupted him, making no attempt to keep their conversation private. 'We quite agree with you. But there is nothing to be done. You must remember that for all these years, in view of the enormous risks and dangers of your profession, you have been privileged to enjoy a very high rate of life insurance cover. This is normal procedure here, and I am sure it was fully explained to you when you joined the *Sûreté*, or else you would never have signed the policy.'

Yes. He remembered now. He had agreed—for his wife's sake—so that she would be well provided for if anything happened to him. Which very often nearly did. But it had all been so long ago. So many years had flown by with such unbelievable rapidity. And now—after them all—he was still alive. Nothing had happened to him. He was standing here in front of this idiot, and the paper in his hand was a joke.

'I see,' he said quietly.

'Good. Come to the table here after the meeting. I will give you the documents for the car. There are a few papers to sign and your gun to hand in. I have nearly finished now.'

'Very well, m'sieu.'

His friend the waiter took one look at his face and promptly handed him an even larger glass of wine.

He then watched in amazement as M. Pinaud drained it in one unbelievable swallow and immediately held it out to him again. In complete silence and with practised dexterity he filled it again.

'Thank you very much.'

For a fleeting moment M. Pinaud felt an urge to confide in this man. Suddenly and inexplicably he felt closer to him than to any other occupant of that crowded room. He was a good type, and sympathetic.

Everyone else around him—Lasaule, the owner of that smug and aggressive voice, M. le Chef, who had delayed getting him a new car until it was too late, even his friends and colleagues the other detectives, because they would continue to draw salaries while he tried to exist on chicken-feed—everyone else in this room was a bastard.

Except this charming waiter, who even now was refilling his glass with swift and imperturbable efficiency.

But that would be childish, Pinaud, he castigated himself with his usual and typical severity. He is a complete stranger, doing his work well and competently. To him, you are just another old bugger getting pissed to drown his misery. What interest can he possibly have in listening to your troubles?

None at all. Leave him. And as soon as this stupid meeting is over go home to see your wife. Well—at least wait until he has finished refilling your glass . . .

Plunged into one of his characteristic moods of profound depression, he stood alone and apart, brooding and drinking.

He was not unduly worried about handing in his gun or signing a few papers. At home he had a veritable arsenal of firearms, acquired without any difficulty over the long years after various desperate encounters with characters who were not likely to need them ever again. It was highly improbable that he would have to use any of them now. If he did, it was only a matter of obtaining a civilian permit. And although he had never cared for paperwork, he knew that he possessed sufficient intelligence to read and understand before he signed.

But somehow it all seemed a sad and insignificant ending to what his chronicler—whose enthusiasm, admiration and respect had never faltered once during all those long and difficult years—still insisted on describing as a great career. Was this how he would have expected it to end? Since he was not in the room, no-one would ever know.

M. Pinaud moodily emptied his glass. He only knew that he had often dreamed it could all have been so different . . .

The friendly waiter, who by now was contemplating him with awe and veneration, hastened to refill it.

Lasaule, in his final brief speech, made it quite clear to the assembled company, without uttering a single word on the subject, that he had now wasted quite enough time and dispensed sufficient free liquor and therefore proposed to get on now with some of the enormous amount of work which he had so confidently undertaken.

Glasses were hastily emptied, farewells said, hands shaken, meaningless and futile platitudes exchanged, and the room began to empty.

M. Pinaud handed in his gun and holster and signed various papers without even bothering to read them. After all, it was hardly likely that the state would try to swindle him at his age—of which he had suddenly become acutely aware.

He looked around unhappily for the man he would always remember as M. le Chef, but he had already gone. He sighed. His chief, in spite of all his manifold faults, had always been a wise man. There was nothing more to say. Everything had been said. This individual in the hideous blue suit would go on saying it for a long time to come—he looked young and healthy enough for that—but it would not be said to him.

He made his way to the car-park. In about an hour and a half, with some really fast driving, he should be home. It was a comforting thought. It would be nice to get into bed.

He unlocked the door, started the engine and lit a cigarette.

Then he sat there for a moment, holding the familiar wheel loosely in his powerful hands. This was now his car, not an employer's. It did not seem in any way different. He had always been provided with a new car periodically, and treated them all with loving care and attention. Each one had therefore seemed as if it were his own personal property. It was a pity this one was so old. If only M. le Chef had listened to him...

He sighed dejectedly. It was too late now. He extinguished his cigarette and drove away through the brightly lit streets and then out into the gathering darkness.

Deliberately he had not telephoned to his wife two days ago when M. le Chef had first shocked him with this news. This was something he would prefer to tell her when they were together. And alone.

She would be upset. She might even cry. Then perhaps he might be of some use. He could be cheerful and joke about it and even make her laugh. He hardly felt like laughing himself, but in the course of his long and arduous career he had learnt that there were very few things a man could not do if he really tried hard enough.

He drove fast, and yet carefully, one part of his mind

trying to think of what he could say to comfort her and with the other reminding himself to cancel the lease of their flat, since he would no longer be able to afford the rent, and wondering at the same time whether they would be compelled to sell the lovely old house they had just paid for and that brought it all back to his wife and the unhappiness he would soon be bringing home to her and the pain and disappointment his news would inevitably cause her . . .

At this juncture in his thoughts, as he saw a straight clear stretch of road ahead and pressed his foot down hard on the accelerator, a strange and disturbing noise suddenly began and continued with sufficient insistence to drive every one of them out of his mind.

Instinctively he slowed up and concentrated on listening. The noise—something compounded of a whine, a vibration and a grind—immediately and definitely diminished, but did not cease. It seemed to come from somewhere behind, in the rear assembly, either from the rear wheel bearings or the back axle or all three together.

He tried accelerating again. The noise immediately increased. Guiltily, he slowed down once more. There was something very wrong at the back. Some bevel wheel or pinion in the back axle was probably badly worn. Or it might be a rear wheel bearing. This was hardly surprising, considering the distance recorded on his speedometer. This had been the theme of all his complaints to M. le Chef for months.

He drove on very slowly. The noise definitely diminished. The slower he went, the more bearable it became. But it was always recognizably there.

The next road sign indicated where he was. Swiftly he considered what he ought to do and then made up his mind—characteristically without hesitation. All-night garages were few and far between on the *autoroute*, and besides, he would soon be turning off at Locroix, along country roads where such things did not exist. It would be more sensible to continue very slowly, without putting any worn part to undue strain and stress, and have the car properly checked in the morning.

Better to arrive late, in spite of his impatience, than to spend the rest of the night in walking or trying to get a lift home from a broken-down and abandoned car.

And so, slowly and sadly and three packets of cigarettes later, he eventually came home to Vervion.

TWO

He had left the main road at Locroix and driven slowly for rather more than half an hour through the rich and rolling countryside. It was now completely dark, but in the glare of his powerful headlights and with the memories of his many visits during the past three months, the scenes before him were as familiar as in daylight.

Vervion was either a large village or a small town, according to one's point of view. He slowed and turned off before he came to the one main High Street, up a narrow lane sign-posted: To the church only. No through road. This lane ended at a group of a few isolated houses adjoining the church.

His new home was on the left, shortly after the signpost. The wide back gate was open, and he turned into the drive, switched off the engine and lights and walked back to close the gate.

For a moment he stood there, feeling the peace and the cool stillness, after the heat and the noise of the city, flowing over his fatigue and tension like a soothing wave of benediction.

The drive led on up through the garden, which

bordered the front and two sides of the house. On his left a copse of tall trees and bushes was bounded by another lane which curved around, bridged the small river and also led to the church past the back of the house.

They had planned to enclose the copse with a fence, since it formed part of their land as far as the adjoining lane. He wondered now whether they would ever be able to afford it.

Then he sighed, took out his latch-key and walked on to the house.

He found Germaine in the front room, looking pathetically frail and vulnerable as she huddled fast asleep in the depths of a capacious armchair. The lights were on and the curtains drawn.

For a long moment he stood there looking down at her, the hard strong lines of his features softened and transfigured with tenderness. Then, with infinite gentleness, he stooped and kissed her brow.

She sighed and stirred, and then awoke with a start.

'Oh—I am so glad to see you. I waited and waited, and then I began to worry that you might have had an accident. And then I must have fallen asleep. I was so tired—I have been gardening all day.'

'I am sorry. There is something wrong with the car, and so I had to creep along like a snail. I should have telephoned you, but it only developed on the road and I was—'

'Never mind.'

She sprang up and into his arms.

'You are back safe and sound. You are here. That is

all that matters. Have you had anything to eat?'

'No. Not much. I am not very hungry. But I could use a drink.'

Now here, in parenthesis, the intelligent reader with a retentive memory will have no difficulty in recalling the amount of wine that M. Pinaud, with the aid of the kind-hearted waiter, had consumed earlier on that evening, and hence might be inclined, with perfect justification, to doubt his chronicler's veracity.

But since that worthy is and always has been only concerned with the truth, the reader in question would be entirely wrong. The explanation is a simple one. It is a fact that all the nervous tension, anxiety and worry he had experienced not only at the *Sûreté* meeting but also on that nightmare drive home, all combined to act together like a catalyst in his veins, burning up and consuming even the not inconsiderable amount of alcohol he had undoubtedly imbibed.

His remark may have sounded strange and unexpected, but it was nevertheless perfectly sincere and completely truthful.

'Nonsense,' she told him severely. 'You must eat something. Remember how you got an ulcer. Go and fix your drink and I will organize the food. There is cold meat and cheese and I can mix you a salad in five minutes. The table is laid.'

'Thank you.'

He went to the cupboard under the stairs and took out one of his last few remaining bottles of absinthe, kept abstemiously and with scrupulous strictness for special occasions and worthy celebrations. And obvioulsy for drowning one's sorrows.

Cold water from the tap, lemon from the larder, a sharp knife from the kitchen drawer, ice from the refrigerator and two glasses from the sideboard—and then he was ready.

When Germaine brought in his food from the kitchen she looked at the brimming second glass with astonishment.

'But you know I only—' she began.

'This is one I think you will need,' he interrupted her quietly. 'I have some rather bad news to tell you. I have known for two days, but I preferred to tell you here, sitting beside you at home, rather than on the telephone.'

At the gravity of his tone she looked at him intently, and then reached out for her glass.

'Go on, then,' she said and took a large swallow.

Briefly and factually, between huge mouthfuls of cold veal and an exquisite salad, he recounted the salient points of his interview with M. le Chef and of his conversation with Lasaule at the meeting.

He came to an end and looked down at his plate, which by dint of a certain amount of talking with his mouth full, he had managed successfully to empty.

'Thank you,' he added. 'That was very nice.'

Then he began to mix himself another drink. Absinthe is a treacherous liquor. It lifts you up very quickly, but drops you down even further. And—in the company of discriminating palates—it is not usually consumed with food.

But M. Pinaud, somewhat naturally, was badly in need of being lifted up, and as he was shortly going to bed, the inevitable and resultant dropping down rather tended to lose both its significance and its importance.

He drank deeply and then wondered moodily why he could find so little enthusiasm for opening a bottle of wine with his cheese.

Germaine looked at him for a long time in silence. Then she lifted her glass and in three enormous and most unladylike swallows emptied it. Which was a fair indication of her consternation.

'You were right,' she said quietly, still looking at him thoughtfully.

'I am usually right,' he replied. 'The trouble is that so few people I meet are willing to admit it.'

It was a simple statement of fact, and not uttered in any spirit of boastfulness.

'But what are we going to do?'

He looked at her and saw that the tears were not very far from her eyes. Impulsively he reached out and took her hand in his own. His clasp was warm and vital and reassuring.

'Now—now,' he said, forcing himself to speak cheerfully. 'The first thing to do is not to worry. You like it here, don't you?'

'The house is a dream and the garden will be the show-place of Vervion when I have finished with it. I have seldom been so happy in all my life.'

'Good. Then we must try to stay. I shall have to see if I can get a job. There is not much money left now.'

'I know. The bill from the builders has just come in. I suppose for nearly three months' work it is justified, but the amount—I nearly fainted when I opened it. And the electric bill for the quarter—we use it here for everything—light, hot water and central heating. How much more will it be in the winter?'

This question he found so terrifying in its implication that he did not dare answer it. Instead he mixed himself another drink.

He held the bottle out towards Germaine, but she shook her head.

'I know,' he said quietly. 'And then there is this nonsense with the car. If there is something worn out, that can cost a lot of money. I must go out and earn some. To-morrow I shall think about it. Just now I am so tired I can't keep my eyes open.'

He smiled at her and took her hand again.

'And you must feel the same—who fell asleep in the armchair? Off you go while I wash up.'

'No—let me—'

'Nonsense. No-one is allowed to do gardening and evening washing up on the same day. Good-night—and promise me to stop worrying. Something will turn up.'

He stood up and took her in his arms.

'Thank you,' she whispered. 'Please let me help—'

'No. Go to bed.'

'Very well. Oh—I am so glad that you are back. There is an awful smell coming from the woodshed. I went myself to see if I could do anything, but there is such a mess in there—'

'I know. That is one of my first jobs before the autumn, to split some logs for the fire and to make it look like a woodshed. But I am not poking about there now with a torch trying to locate a smell. First thing in the morning—I promise you. Now go to bed. I will not be long. Good-night and sleep well.'

He slept deeply and profoundly, which was hardly surprising, and awoke feeling refreshed, energetic and confident.

After all, he had not lived for so many years without absorbing one or two of life's simpler lessons. He knew that a large proportion of the things he had worried about had never happened. And he knew that however arduous and difficult a task might appear to his vivid imagination, hard work and determination inevitably made it easier.

He got up early and quietly, leaving Germaine still fast asleep in bed, made his own breakfast, and immediately afterwards went out to the woodshed, one of a line of ancient and decaying buildings added on originally as stables to part of the back of the house.

Their half-doors sagged, but still closed. There were latches against the wind, but no padlocks. The first and largest one, opposite the back door, they used for garden tools, deck-chairs and dustbins. The next one held wire-netting and an assorted collection of planks, stakes and poles. Then came the woodshed, and finally the last one with boxes, shelves and tables for storing fruit.

In all of them he had looked forward to spending happy and contented hours when he found the time, cleaning them and repairing them and tidying up all their contents to his own meticulous and perfectionist satisfaction. He could even mend the doors and wire an electric light in each.

As he opened the two half-doors of the woodshed the emanating smell effectively interrupted all these thoughts.

The inside was a mess—logs, branches, kindling and broken boxes all piled up in a gigantic confusion which offended his tidy and methodical nature.

A chopping-block stood in one corner. Leaning against it were a long woodsman's axe, a small hatchet and a cross-saw. In the other corner stood two large and battered packing-cases, split and riddled with woodworm, obviously destined to be chopped for firewood.

It was from one of these that the smell was definitely emanating. It was strange, he thought, because if some small animal had climbed and fallen in, why was the lid still on? There was no lid on the adjoining case, which contained only a pile of miscellaneous rubbish in the bottom.

It might be some kind of fungus growth—these could smell very unpleasantly, he had heard. Or it could be some rotting and decaying vegetable matter, emptied in error into the case instead of on the compost heap.

But at this juncture, speculation was a waste of time. The thing to do was to find out.

Wondering, he lifted the lid. It was neither animal nor fungus. And even if it had begun to decay, the matter was definitely not vegetable.

Doubled up inside, knees to chin, was the dead body of a young girl.

He stepped forward, bent down, and lifted her out by her shoulders, tenderly and with care, and yet in one powerful heave. Then he laid the dead body on the grass outside and kneeling down, composed it decently

Her features were peaceful. His mind, after a lifetime of experience with violent death, ranged rapidly and efficiently over some of the possibilities.

There was a bruise on the side of her jaw, but she had been killed by a blow on her head, probably with the back of the small hatchet inside. The nature of the wound was consistent with such an instrument, and moreover, it was lying handy.

He had noticed an old pair of working gloves beside the chopping-block. Standing up, he re-entered the shed and picked up the hatchet very carefully by the edge of its blade. One glance at the back of its head confirmed that his theory was correct.

It would be a waste of time looking for fingerprints on the handle. She must have been induced to go into the woodshed, knocked out by one swift blow to the jaw and then the gloves put on to handle the hatchet.

Or there might not even have been need for inducement. The blow could have been struck outside while passing the doors and the unconscious body carried in.

But when? People are not usually murdered in other people's woodsheds, he reflected, or even outside them, unless they had both come into the garden at night. But then how could a murderer ever have persuaded his prospective victim to walk in someone else's garden at night?

Throughout the day, Germaine was usually in the garden, since the weather had been consistently fine, and the builders had been working on the roof and painting the outside walls. They would have seen. They would have noticed.

Unless it had been on a Sunday morning, when

Germaine always went to church and builders did not work. That was more likely. From the smell she must have been dead for about a week. And a normal Sunday morning walk, up the lane and through the copse into the deserted garden, to see how the builders were getting on with the old house—that was far more likely. That was something in which any young girl might have shown interest.

He went outside again and knelt beside the body.

Both from the features and from the gaily-striped dress she wore, he recognized her without difficulty. Her name was Louise Voisin. She was a local girl, who earned a living by representing a firm of household suppliers in Locroix, travelling around locally as an agent on commission.

She had called at the house several times during the past few months, usually at the week-end, having found out from the local grape-vine that this was the best time to see him and his wife together.

She had showed them brushes and mops, dish-cloths and scourers, tins of polish and wax. New heads for brooms, new brushes for carpet-sweepers, tins of detergent, bleach and washing-up liquid—in short, everything that they would need to keep the house clean.

Germaine had been polite, but firm. She had told her that they were still in the process of moving in, and with the builders still in the house she had as yet no definite idea of her requirements. She would be grateful if Mademoiselle Voisin could call in again in about a month's time, when they would be pleased to give her an order. At the present moment, with builders walking all over the house, she really did not know whether she was coming or going. When they had finally finished, things should be easier.

Louise Voisin had smiled cheerfully, assured them that she fully understood the position, and promised to call again later.

She promptly appeared again in a week's time, and thereafter called once a week, listening attentively to Germaine's almost identical speeches. She did not insist on showing any of her goods again, but merely smiled knowingly and hoped that they would soon be ready to buy.

She had been an attractive and charming person, he remembered, with an impish, provocative and definitely sexual smile.

And now she was dead. He sighed and murmured a prayer for the young life so tragically ended.

Then he stood up, found a large tin of disinfectant in one of the sheds, which he emptied into the packing-case, and then went indoors, first to wash his hands thoroughly in more disinfectant, secondly to telephone the local police, and thirdly to take Germaine a cup of coffee and tell her what had happened.

The voice at the other end of the telephone had sounded calm, crisp and efficient. Within an astonishingly short time a burly policeman had driven a closed van up the drive and the body had been swiftly and unobtrusively removed.

And M. Pinaud's appointment with Inspector Javel was for two o'clock.

Moodily he stood outside the woodshed, contemplated the wide-open half-doors, sniffed the strong odour of disinfectant and wondered what had happened to his earlier feeling of energy and confidence.

There was so much work to be done here he did not know where to begin. Quite apart from tidying up the sheds, the lawns had to be cut, the vegetable garden dug and weeded, and dead branches sawn off in the copse for winter firewood.

Germaine had quite enough to do with her flower-beds, her half-tubs and hanging baskets, with which she had created such a lovely show of colour outside the house. It was only right and fitting, he thought, that he should do all he could to help.

Besides, the vintage motor mower he had bought from the previous owner was decidedly temperamental, and starting it up, by means of a hand-cord, had proved beyond her powers. That was another thing he would have to do. Clean and lubricate it, fit a new sparking-plug and new blades to the rotar-arm, and change the oil in the sump, so that she could use it herself when he was not there.

But all these things would have to wait. The reek of disinfectant was definitely better than last night's objectionable smell, but he could not bring himself to go into the woodshed again. Not just now. When he had time and felt better he would take the long-handled axe and break up that packing-case for firewood. Broken and shattered planks would not torment his vivid imagination so horribly with images of that pathetic body he had lifted from the inside of their assembly.

But now there was something more important to do.

He had to take his car to the local garage.

If he had not been completely convinced, over the past few months, that within a matter of weeks or even days M. le Chef would see reason and order him a new car, he might well have hesitated before finalizing the purchase of their new house.

This, after months of intensive searching, had proved to be their dream house. It had Germaine's idea of what a garden should be. They were both completely and ecstatically happy at the thought of living in it.

But the house was situated in Vervion, whose railway station had been closed some twenty years previously, since the branch-line no longer paid. There was a primitive bus-service to Locroix, twice a day, at the most inconvenient times imaginable.

A car here was not a luxury, but a necessity. Without one, how could he continue to earn his living?

As yet, he had not decided what he was going to do. But it was almost certain that he would have to try in Locroix, which was a town large enough to offer possibilities. It was not likely that there would be any openings in Vervion for an erstwhile famous and celebrated detective. It was reasonable to assume that Inspector Javel was fully capable of coping with whatever local crime was rampant.

So if he went to work in Locroix he would need a car, if only to get him there in time in the morning and bring him home at night.

It was not a matter of making a decision, but of accepting facts. The decision had already been made by Henri Lasaule and his merry and well related young men.

Victorin Dufour owned the local garage in the High Street. He was a short stocky individual, dark and swarthy, with immense shoulders and a barrel-like chest, all three of which strained the buttons of the immaculate white coat he wore.

He listened sympathetically to M. Pinaud's tale of woe, wiping his hands meticulously on a clean piece of rag. Then he walked across the forecourt towards the car.

'May I see the engine, m'sieu?' he asked politely.

The voice that issued from that mighty chest was incongruously soft and gentle. Wondering, M. Pinaud released the catch and pulled up the bonnet. He had mentioned the words, back axle and rear wheels, at least six times. Why look at the wrong end, then? Any mechanic, by looking at the car, would know that it did not have front-wheel drive. Surely the first thing to do would have been to—

Dufour, who had been contemplating the engine carefully, interrupted his train of thought without compunction.

'Before I undertake any work on any car, M'sieu, I always ask to see the engine,' he explained. 'That tells me exactly how the car has been treated. I have seldom seen one so beautifully clean as this. It pleases me to look at it. And it pleases me to congratulate you.'

He lowered and closed the bonnet gently, without slamming it, and a sudden smile seemed to illuminate his dark and swarthy features.

'Since you seem to have a certain difficulty in finding words to describe this noise, m'sieu, the obvious thing is for me to listen to it myself. Provided you have no

objection?'
'Of course not.'
'Good. Excuse me while I get a cushion.'
Had he delayed, M. Pinaud might have begun to wonder again, but he was back in a moment. The cushion was old, but as clean as his coat. He put it on the driving-seat and got in. Feeling underneath, he released the adjustment lever and ran the seat forward to its fullest extent.
'That is better,' he said. 'This model is too low and too long for one of my shape.'
M. Pinaud, who had climbed in beside him, watched his one swift and expert glance that took in everything on the instrument panel.
'Right around the clock, I presume?'
'Twice,' he replied.
Dufour stared at him.
'It was an official car. I had to go everywhere. Now I have just retired. It has been presented to me. I am unable to afford a new one, so I am hoping that it will go around three times.'
Dufour waited to reply until he had started the engine and driven the car out of the forecourt. In the High Street he accelerated, and then turned his head slightly to one side as the noise started and he listened.
'No hope at all with this noise,' he said shortly.
He braked and turned off at the cross-roads. In a few moments they had left the last house behind, and the peaceful undulating countryside, with its fields and hedges and isolated farms, streamed past on either side.
Hitherto M. Pinaud had always prided himself on

his ability to drive a car not only rapidly but competently.

Now he felt like a novice. This one was a master. After a few moments he was profoundly impressed. After a few more he was terrified. He wondered whether he should shut his eyes or pray, or both.

Their speed, unbelievably, continued to increase. The road was a second-class one and narrow. Dufour seemed to think that he was on the *autoroute*.

The noise, strangely enough, although louder, had not increased as much as he would have expected.

'I was always told,' he ventured diffidently—after an aged man driving a tractor had obligingly mounted a steep bank to give them a half-centimetre clearance as they flashed past—'I was told, not once but many times, that the only way to negotiate these country roads is to keep well in to the side—'

'No side on this one,' Dufour interrupted him cheerfully. 'Much too narrow. And I have to listen to this noise at speed. Besides, I know where everyone is going to be at this time of day.'

And to prove his point, breath-takingly, his glance left the road to look at the watch on his wrist.

M. Pinaud shuddered, but made a great and praiseworthy effort to control himself. After all, this one was trying to help him, and there was always a profound satisfaction in being with someone capable and confident, and obviously master of his trade.

Mercifully, and perhaps even because of this, the ordeal soon came to an end.

Dufour suddenly slowed, braked and stopped. Then he reversed the car into the entrance to a farmer's field and drove back sedately to Vervion.

'I am sure I have a good idea now of what it might be,' he said. 'It is definitely due to wear—either a wheel in the differential or a bearing or both—but the only way to locate it to make sure is to dismantle the back axle. And that is a big job, m'sieu. Even if I start it now, it will take a day or two. I only have one foreman and a boy to help me.'

M. Pinaud closed his eyes. For a moment he could not help feeling sad. It was no surprise to hear that his beloved car was old and worn out. Since yesterday—for the first time in his life—he had begun to feel the same himself.

But to him, perhaps because of the dangers and perils of his profession, a car had always been something more than a mere mass of metal. It assumed a personality of its own. He washed it, cleaned it, polished it, looked after it, and even—after some long hair-raising chase at an illegal speed—had been known to speak to it and thank it before switching off the engine . . .

With the instantaneous wonder of thought, visions and memories of the past flashed through his mind—scenes where in this car his skill and reckless driving had made possible the saving of a life and the capture of a criminal—scenes of miraculous and hair's-breadth escapes from death on the road, and scenes where only his will and iron determination to succeed had triumphed over his fatigue and kept his mastery of the wheel . . .

It was so easy to feel sad. But self-pity never did any man any good. He opened his eyes and came back to the present.

'It must be done,' he said quietly. 'I would be very grateful if you will do what is necessary.'

'Very well. I think you are wise. Far better we should find the trouble on our hoist rather than having something seize up on the main road when you are in a hurry. The rust on the bodywork I would advise you to leave until later. It is bad enough, but it could be worse. That too, can be a very costly job, because of the time involved. You will already have enough expense with your back axle.'

M. Pinaud looked at him with a new respect. No-one had mentioned rust. In that brief moment when he had walked towards the car, Dufour had noticed and seen the patches at the base of the doors, the front wings and the boot.

And yet, because of what he had said, he seemed to be genuinely trying to help, and not to make his invoice bigger. Here, it seemed, he had found a type rare in this modern world—an honest man. His gratitude was evident in his voice.

'That is very kind of you, M'sieu Dufour. I appreciate your advice and the spirit in which it is given.'

They had not gone a great distance. Soon they were back in the forecourt.

As M. Pinaud got out, he noticed that the main workshed was being lengthened and enlarged, and a new path was being laid by several builders to connect up to the sliding doors at the far end. In the centre of the forecourt another workman was hammering the last nails into a new wooden sign. Its wording was neat and courteous:

Thank you for your custom. Please come again to the family firm of Dufour.

'Business is good, then?' he ventured. 'You are expanding?'

Dufour got out and closed the door carefully and quietly before he replied. Then he smiled again.

'Yes. I have more work here than I can manage. I shall have to employ another mechanic. The trouble is these days to find a good and conscientious one. The young men to-day are not trained as I was. But I shall continue to supervise and check everything myself, as I have always done. We are forming a new company—my wife, my son and I. He is finishing his course soon at the engineering school. He will be concentrating on the second-hand sales. There are great opportunities to-day—if one is prepared to accept and keep to a few basic principles.'

'I am sure you are right. I wish you good luck.'

'Thank you, m'sieu. May I ask if you have finally settled in now?'

'Of course. The answer is yes. There is still a lot of work, but the builders have finished.'

'Good. And do you think you will like it here in Vervion?'

'We do not even have to think. We are certain.'

'Good again. I am sorry to hear that you have had some trouble this morning.'

M. Pinaud stared.

'But how could you possibly—'

The smile broadened as Dufour interrupted him.

'This is a small place, m'sieu. We all know what is

going on. In some ways that can be a good thing—in others not.'

M. Pinaud began to wonder vaguely which side of this equivocal decision might affect him, when he realized that Dufour was holding out his hand and talking about something entirely different.

'I have left the seat, my cushion, and the key in the lock, m'sieu, as I shall be driving your car myself on to the hoist very shortly. Look in to-morrow or whenever you are passing and I will let you know how we are getting on.'

'Thank you very much. I will do that.'

They shook hands ceremoniously, since this was obviously expected.

M. Pinaud reflected that throughout his career he had never shaken hands with a garage-man in Paris. He decided that in spite of all his troubles he was going to like it here in Vervion. There was something quaintly fascinating and appealing about this small place where everyone knew exactly what was happening to everyone else in such an incredibly short time.

He wondered whether this omniscience might extend as far as the identity of the individual who had decided to murder Louise Voisin in his woodshed. If not, he would have to do something about that himself.

THREE

Inspector Javel was tall and powerfully built, with dark saturnine features and completely expressionless pale grey eyes. He was wearing a beautifully cut suit and a very expensive shirt whose cuffs were fastened by massive gold links.

Even sitting behind his desk in that plain and bleak office on the first floor he seemed to radiate a dominating competence which was as unmistakable as it was impressive.

'Ah, yes—M'sieu Pinaud,' he said, waving a hand towards the other chair in front of the desk. 'Please sit down.'

His voice as deep and resonant, his diction clear and precise, and as they continued to speak, his phrases proved to be well turned and expressive. Altogether, M. Pinaud reflected, quite an unusual figure to be sitting at the desk of a local police-station in a small and obscure place like Vervion.

He did not stand nor offer to shake hands, which fact M. Pinaud, brought up in a tradition of old-fashioned courtesy, found somewhat perturbing.

'Thank you,' he replied, and sat down.

'I have heard of your exploits in the past.'

This too, was strange. Despite all his illusions, dreams and desires, M. Pinaud still remained something of a realist. It was highly unlikely, in spite of his chronicler's praise-worthy and heart-breaking efforts for so many years, that anyone in this remote part of the world had ever heard of him and the lifetime of conscientious toil he had dedicated to make his career a success.

'I mean to say,' the inspector continued, 'In Locroix —not here. We too, have been having purges there just like you in the *Sûreté*. I was sent here pending some considerable re-organization, which after a year is still going on.'

This made it all easier to understand, but the inspector did not smile as he spoke. This was clearly to be an official interview and not a social occasion. There was also a definite if unexpressed feeling of hostility, which his sensitive awareness to atmosphere recognized without difficulty, even if he could not understand it.

He therefore did not answer, but waited politely for the inspector to continue.

'A few general remarks before we begin. This is a very small town, hardly more than a village, where everybody knows everyone else. It is vastly different from Locroix, but I have found no difficulty in applying the same principles of order and method which made a success of my administration there.

'I patrol this place very often, as frequently as I can. Yours is the last house after the church. I go as far as that. Even young boys on bicycles hesitate to throw stones at windows if they have the impression that they are being watched. In this way crime can usually be prevented before it happens.'

'But this one did,' M. Pinaud remarked.

'Exactly. Yours is the first crime—'

'Why do you say yours?' M. Pinaud interrupted.

The inspector frowned. It was obviously not done to interrupt him when he was speaking.

'Because it happened in your woodshed and you discovered the body. That made it yours. Now it becomes mine. I told you that I am awaiting promotion either in Locroix or an even larger town. You can imagine my feelings at having an unsolved crime here in Vervion.'

There was a pause. M. Pinaud stirred in his chair.

'You say unsolved—' he began.

Swiftly the inspector demonstrated that the right of interruption in this room belonged to him alone.

'Yes. I used the word deliberately, advisedly, and with reason. This is more than likely to remain an unsolved crime. But let us begin at the beginning and not at the end. The dead body was that of Louise Voisin, a young local girl aged twenty.'

'I know that,' M. Pinaud told him.

'We all know that you know that. The fact is hardly surprising, since she called on everyone here as an agent for her firm of household goods.'

He took up a paper from his desk and looked at it.

'Doctor Poidevin, our local doctor, acts as police surgeon for us when necessary. I have here his report of the autopsy. She was struck unconscious by a blow, presumably from a man's clenched fist, and then killed by a second one with the head of an axe on the back of her skull. Death would have been instantaneous. She did not suffer. Doctor Poidevin is still working on the time of death, trying to narrow it down even further, but that is a long process involving the examination of many of the organs. However, he is reasonably certain already that it happened less than a week ago. Probably last Sunday. It could well have been last Sunday.'

'Why do you say that?' M. Pinaud asked him.

'Because this all points to a local crime. Someone—it is common knowledge—knew that you have had builders working all day for weeks on your roof, from which they could easily see your woodshed. Someone has observed your wife working in her new garden, now that the weather has turned fine. And everyone here knows that she has gone to church every Sunday morning since she moved in.

And it is also common knowledge that builders do not work on a Sunday. Very few people here leave their houses on that day. In the summer they tend their gardens. In the winter there are odd jobs to be done indoors. He probably did not even need to risk being seen with her. He could have arranged to walk alone through the copse and to meet her in your garden, perhaps to see what a wonderful renovation the builders have done on your old house.'

'I thought all that out for myself,' M. Pinaud told him quietly. 'As soon as I found the body.'

For the first time the inspector looked at him with something that could have been interest and might even have been respect.

'You did? That was good thinking. And so there will

be no witness to come forward to swear that they were seen together. If she was seen alone—what does that signify? She was always out. And any man might have been noticed walking alone towards the copse. Each one will have a legitimate reason, even though one of them is a murderer. You understand now why I referred to it as an unsolved crime.'

There was silence for a moment. Then the inspector took up the paper again.
'Now let us come back to the beginning,' he said. 'Louise Voisin was three months pregnant when she died.'
He paused and looked up, as if expecting some comment. M. Pinaud did not make any.
'This news did not surprise me,' the inspector continued. 'She was completely promiscuous. She was also young and wild, and came from a broken home. Which means that she lacked the restraining influence of good parents when she was young. In addition she was a person with an extraordinary sexual attraction. Had she lived she might have ended up more or less as the town tart.
'Not for money—or else I might have made a case of it and removed her to a larger place like Locroix—but she was promiscuous because of the sheer joy she got out of copulation. You occasionally get people like that. She was more than over-sexed—she was the very incarnation of sex. She had a habit of looking you up and down and undressing you with her eyes—you knew exactly what she was thinking and estimating and calculating. Then suddenly she would smile. And

her smile told you definitely how right you had been.'

He paused for a moment and laid the paper down.

'I would say,' he resumed, 'That since she was at school, she has had intercourse at some time or other with the majority of the male population here in Vervion, regardless of age or social station.'

Here, surprisingly, the inspector used words to denote explicitly the certain unmistakable parts of the male and female anatomy which would have been employed to confirm his statement—words which M. Pinaud knew without a doubt not only his chronicler but also his publisher would inevitably censor.

Therefore, with the experience of age and with a fitting consideration for the laborious task these two gentlemen had undertaken together in bringing his exploits before the public, he took it upon himself to alter his own notes before even writing them.

'Not for money, mind you,' the inspector was saying, 'But just for the sheer love and joy of the sexual act. She was that kind of person. As I said before—completely promiscuous. Although, in all fairness to her, everyone will confirm that she seemed to be settling down nicely in her new job.'

He paused again and then clasped his hands together.

'This is obviously a case of murder. But I prefer to think of it as suicide. According to this evidence, she committed suicide when she decided to blackmail someone in this place for being the father of her child.'

M. Pinaud, with considerably more years of experience than the inspector, had arrived at this same conclusion immediately he had heard of Louise

Voisin's pregnancy, but he was interested in hearing what the man would say next, so he contented himself with looking suitably impressed and made the right answer.

'Blackmail—but how—why? If she was promiscuous—'

'Be patient. I will tell you. And in telling you, this will at once give me a list of suspects. Any average man, knowing her reputation, might have laughed in her face, and told her to contact some of the other men she had been sleeping with—but not here.

'Here in Vervion we have a number of reputable citizens, who could never afford to risk the publicity involved in even trying to deny the paternity of her child. Not only respectably married men, but young ones with careers and objectives in front of them.

'I think at once of our Doctor Poidevin. He is a brilliant young man, and extremely ambitious, but this job he has here is only a stepping-stone to higher things. He makes no secret of it. I happen to know that after a day's hard work he studies until very late every night, preparing for his examinations to gain admittance as senior pathologist at one of the major Paris hospitals. Can you imagine the effect on his chances of qualifying if he had to appear in a local court to deny paternity charges?'

He looked at M. Pinaud but did not wait for an answer to his question.

'Whether they were true or false is in no way pertinent. It is the publicity that would ruin all his chances, destroy his hopes and wreck his career. For this reason he therefore automatically becomes suspect.

'His wife is a similar type—as young and as ambitious as he is. They are not well liked here. The local people resent a manner which indicates only too clearly that they know they are both destined for higher things. Talk and gossip would not only be inevitable, but even malicious, because of this resentment. You are with me so far, M'sieu Pinaud?'

'Yes. I see what you mean.'

'And without any difficulty I can think of another one. General Correvon. Retired here after a distinguished career in the Army. He came to this office about ten days ago to complain. He said he wanted me to warn her unofficially. Which I did. After all, he is a respected and distinguished citizen.

'But by then it was already to late. I should think she had already been around to everyone concerned. She just laughed in my face and said she had done nothing wrong and never even mentioned the word blackmail. All she had done was to have a few preliminary conversations with certain gentlemen who might have some interest in becoming the father of her child.

'I could do nothing. The general took pains to assure me that he was not making an official complaint, but merely trying to protect a young and foolish girl from what might be the dangerous consequences of her folly.

'That is why I know there must have been blackmail.

'Now one of the oldest and best established of all military axioms—and the most respected—is the one that states attack is the best defence. And General Correvon is one of the old school. He said he warned her that she was on a dangerous course and told her that if she came to see him again he would notify the police. This time officially.

'Of course, he might have been bluffing. There is always a feint attack before every major offensive.

'He lives in the large white house on the other side of the church. A general's pension is really something, I can assure you. I only hope that his wife was not there when he received his visitor. She is a querulous and complaining woman who spends all her spare time in using her family's connections and influence with the Minister to get her husband appointed to the post of Resident Governor somewhere in a better climate than Normandy.

'So far she has not been successful. But they are still hopeful. It is a well-known fact that the War Office, when considering senior appointments, do not look kindly on blackmail.'

The inspector paused for a moment, either to reassure himself that his thoughts were still in their orderly sequence or else to give M. Pinaud a chance to comment upon his remarks.

His visitor opened his mouth to speak and then closed it again. There was no point in asking questions. He did not know either of these people. On the other hand, he found the inspector's brief but vivid character-sketches completely fascinating and therefore continued to listen with interest.

'There are two more I would like to mention. Robert Macon is one. He started going out with Louise Voisin while they were still at school. He was wild then. They made a fit pair. He did not have to teach her very much.

'About that time there were a series of burglaries from some of the larger houses here. When I read my predecessor's notes about them I immediately thought of young Robert. How else would Louise have found the money to rent and furnish her flat? Certainly not from her family.

'But there was never any proof. Robert might have been young, but he had a brilliant brain. He did what he wanted, planned and organized each entry with the precision of a mathematical problem, obviously went to Paris to dispose of the jewellery at one-tenth of its value with no questions asked, got the money he needed and left no clues. And so there could not be any charges and the file was closed.

'But as young Robert grew up an extraordinary thing happened. He controlled his wildness and decided to work and use his brain to become a respectable citizen. He saw less of Louise—which did not seem to worry her. She was fully occupied in making new contacts.

'Robert Macon is now managing his father's family business, the general clothing store at the end of the High Street, and making a great success of it. He has settled down into an ambitious and capable executive, and apparently has some very interesting plans for expansion by opening a chain of similar shops in various local towns.

'He would not like the idea of blackmail or marriage very much, I can assure you. To expand in business one needs capital. Money can easily be borrowed, but the question of character references usually arises.

Besides, he is far too busy to have time for a wife. He would have married her long ago had he wanted to. He preferred to enjoy his sex-life at a time when it was the most important thing in the world. Thanks to Louise, he was able to do this without any of the normal responsibilities which sometimes can make it so difficult.'

Again the inspector paused. M. Pinaud decided it was time he demonstrated that he had been listening carefully and that his memory was retentive.

'And the other one?' he asked quietly.

'Armand Brissac, our local jeweller and watch-repairer. You have seen his lovely old house in the High Street, with its projecting upper floor and moulded door?'

'Yes. But I have had no occasion to go in.'

'Nor have most people here, except for repairs. When there is a birthday or an anniversary to celebrate, most of them go to Locroix, where the shops have modern displays and are well stocked. His one small window with its leaded panes of blown glass may well be seven hundred years old, but what he has in it is a joke. Leather watch-straps and alarm-clocks, as you will have noticed.

'He inherited the business from his father and grandfather, who both did quite well for themselves in those days when transport was not so easy. But I know for a fact that he has already spent most of their money. He buys gold and spends most of his spare time in making rings which are too expensive to sell. He does not even put them in that window of his.

'Yet I believe that he is a happy man—in so far as any creative artist can be happy when he is not working. Blackmail—either money or marriage, whichever she wanted—would have wrecked his life. Paying out money would have prevented him from buying gold. And like most artists, he would not have made a good husband.'

The inspector leaned back in his chair and contemplated M. Pinaud carefully. There was still no expression in the pale grey eyes.

'And there are others, M'sieu Pinaud,' he continued evenly. 'These are just the ones that come first to my mind. I propose to interview and question them all officially. That is my duty.

'And there is one more. Yes—quite definitely there is one more. This will not be easy.'

He paused for a moment to reflect.

'Now we must approach this problem logically and in accordance with the best and classic traditions of detection. This is something which I am sure you yourself, M'sieu Pinaud, will be the first to appreciate.'

There was another pause, this time longer. The inspector raised his hands, placed his fingertips carefully together and looked at them instead of at M. Pinaud.

'You remember I told you that Louise Voisin was three months pregnant when she died?'

'Yes.'

'In fact, that is just about the time you and your wife moved into your new house, is it not?'

'Yes.'

The echoes of M. Pinaud's second affirmative

seemed to him to resound in the silence that ensued long after he had spoken.

The inspector's features were impassive, his eyes expressionless. Even his words were uninflected—and therefore all the more startling in their implication . . . M. Pinaud was incredulous.

'You—you must be joking,' he said at length.

'Not at all. This is not a subject for joking. Apparently she called on you several times as soon as you were in to try to sell you something.'

'Naturally. She was an agent. We were potential clients. But obviously we were far too busy. We told her to call back once we had settled in.'

'She is, unfortunately, hardly in a position to confirm that.'

M. Pinaud was out of his chair and standing up in a second.

'You mean that I am lying?'

The Inspector did not react. He did not even move.

'At the present moment,' he replied quietly, 'I do not mean anything. I am merely including you, as is my right, in the summary I have taken the trouble to give you of other people in this office just now.'

He lowered his fingertips and stared calmly at M. Pinaud, still without expression, as he continued.

'For example, I would add that your financial situation is probably not too good to-day—you have had to retire unexpectedly from the *Sûreté* because of this new purge. Therefore you are no longer paid a salary, whatever it was in the past. They are known to be notoriously mean at the *Quai d'Orsai*. And then you will be receiving a very large bill in a short while—the builders have been at your house for more than three months.'

M. Pinaud still stood, amazed and angry. He found the very words hard to believe.

'You seem to know a good deal about me, Inspector Javel.'

'That is my duty. And we all know a good deal about the *Sûreté*—even in a small town like this—and about you. Your exploits—I will not say have become famous —but are certainly beginning to become more widely known.'

He paused, and for a moment there was silence. M. Pinaud did not break it. He could hardly be expected, after a lifetime of endeavour, to refute such a statement.

The inspector continued to speak:

'And in nearly all of them—now here is the true significance of my remark—there is always some stark-naked young girl who plays a prominent part. Perhaps you found one when you came here. Louise Voisin would have had no inhibitions, qualms nor objections with regard to taking all her clothes off—she did it often enough before.'

The inspector paused again. M. Pinaud waited. He could find no words. The whole situation seemed to have taken on a strange and unreal—almost dreamlike —quality. It was as if he were standing there in the throes of a nightmare, watching two other people, of which he was one, but powerless to speak or interfere. This could not be happening to him.

'I told you at once, M'sieu Pinaud,' he heard the inspector saying, 'That immediately I could think of a list of suspects for this crime. And there may even be others. The local garagist, Dufour, for instance, now also comes to my mind. He has wife trouble, because she has the money he needs for his expansion. And she has a mother, who never did think much of her marriage. I may say here and now that nearly all the local married men of your age, respectable and with the dignity of a position in society to maintain, are automatically suspect. It stands to reason.

'And now you yourself are a local resident as well And like one or two of the others, you are almost certainly at a very difficult sex-age. Desire—with all its attendant problems—usually dies down with the passing of time. But not always. It can often be aroused and stimulated—even perverted—by a provocative and erotic young girl.'

M. Pinaud made a great effort to rouse himself and break this fantastic spell.

'Inspector Javel,' he said hardly, 'You are talking utter cock and nonsense. With my wife moving in to a new house and all her problems of curtains and carpets —and with me only able to come to see her and help her on occasional week-ends—how on earth do you think I would have had the time—let alone the opportunity—'

Inspector Javel interrupted him.

'That is not my problem.'

'Then what is?'

'Mine is that each and every one of these people I am going to interview and question will certainly have an alibi. There is as yet no evidence—apart from the fact that it was your hand-axe—which we have taken and are keeping—which was used. Therefore I am not making any statements at this stage. I am not condemning nor accusing anyone. I am only trying to find an explanation for a particularly brutal and unnecessary murder. And to keep an open mind.'

M. Pinaud relaxed and sat down. There was really nothing else to do. What the inspector had said was fair and reasonable enough.

He thought for a moment and then spoke.

'You said that it happened very probably last Sunday.'

'Yes.'

'Then that lets me out. I did not come home last Sunday.'

'I know that.'

'How?'

'Sometimes I patrol on Sunday afternoons as well as in the week. Your wife went to church in the morning and spent the afternoon gardening.'

'As I said—you seem to know a good deal about other people.'

'Yes. It is my duty.'

The inspector paused for a moment and then continued to speak, without any change in the inflection of his voice.

'And I also know that you have a very fast car, even if it is getting old. The distance from Paris is not so great, and the *autoroute* is a good one. And by now, after all your visits here during the past three months, you will surely know what time our church service starts and what time it ends.'

Again he paused, but this time he did not continue.

The silence seemed to hang heavily between them until M. Pinaud ended it.

'What are you trying to tell me, Inspector Javel?'

There was still nothing to be read in those pale and expressionless eyes.

'Nothing of any great consequence. I have given you a list of likely suspects and told you the reasons why it is not complete. All I have to do now is to interview each one and then be patient and wait.'

'I wish I could do the same.'

'What do you mean?'

'There is no need to tell you how much you have upset me.'

'I am sorry. I try to do my duty.'

'It is gratifying to hear your apology—but I do not believe it.'

'As you wish.'

The words were indifferent and unconcerned.

'You are going to question all these people?'

'Yes. From the way they answer certain of my questions I might learn something.'

'I intend to ask them questions as well.'

'Why?'

'If only to clear myself of your suspicions.'

'That is both laudable and commendable. But you will not find that easy.'

'Why not?'

'Because you have no legal status here to do such a thing. May I remind you that you are no longer a renowned detective, but a retired detective. You may find it different. You will certainly find it difficult.'

'I am used to difficulties.'

'So I have gathered from your exploits. You are not thinking of leaving us, are you?'

Their stares seemed to lock and hold.

'No. I am not thinking of leaving Vervion. My wife and I have dreamed of a house like this for a very long time. Not even your suspicions, Inspector Javel, can make us give it up now.'

'They are not my suspicions, M'sieu Pinaud. You of all people should know and appreciate that. I am paid to do my duty. I try to do it well and earn my salary honestly. That does not stop me from wishing you good luck.'

To his own intense astonishment M. Pinaud found himself standing up, shaking hands and thanking the inspector.

As he left the office he wondered why and for what.

FOUR

M. Pinaud addressed the proprietor of The Seven Sons of Aymon with conviction, confidence, sincerity, authority and charm—all together simultaneously blended in his voice.

'Good-afternoon to you, m'sieu. I would like a pot of very strong black coffee. And I feel that I need something even stronger to go with it. I have been told that in this district some of the local farmers have their own ways of dealing with surplus apples. I am sure that you would—'

The proprietor held up his hand to silence him, his huge face, a fitting crowning for his elephantine body, wreathed in smiles.

'Say no more, m'sieu. You have come to the right place. Just be patient for a few moments.'

He left the counter and walked towards the back of the *café*, the plank flooring of the small building groaning and vibrating under his implacable and relentless tread.

He was as good as his word. In a very short while the thudding and protesting timbers heralded his return, a steaming coffee-pot balanced on a tray in one massive hand, the other clutching a squat hand-blown glass bottle firmly by the neck.

He set down the tray on the table, poured the coffee with a twist and a flourish, pushed the cream jug towards the cup and felt in his pocket for a corkscrew.

'It is a pleasure to welcome you to my *café*, M'sieu Pinaud,' he said as he proceeded to open the bottle with considerable skill and the minimum of effort.

M. Pinaud was surprised. This was the first time he had been inside the *café*.

'You know my name?'

'Of course, m'sieu. Your charming wife has been shopping here in the High Street for some three months. In a small place like Vervion, everyone knows everyone else.'

'This I am beginning to believe,' M. Pinaud told him, and watched with interest as the pale colourless liquid was carefully poured into a large wine-glass, filling it to the brim.

'There, m'sieu. A liqueur distilled by one of our local farmers. This bottle has been in my cellar for three years. The secret of any home-distilled brew lies in the maturing. This is my trade. I flatter myself I know it well. I should do—since my father taught me everything that he had learnt from my grandfather.'

Here he took a damp cloth from his pocket and wiped the already immaculate table.

'This will cost you ten francs for a small measure and twenty for this. But in these days of inflation, when everything costs more and is usually of inferior quality, it represents a remarkable bargain, even at this price. Please judge for yourself.'

M. Pinaud needed no urging. He proceeded to do so. He took one careful sip, and then, intoxicated by the fragrant aroma and delicious taste, another sip followed by a gigantic swallow.

He had the sudden sensation that it would be easy to imagine the back of his head had been blown off. This drink was fantastic. Its strength was diabolical, its impact incredible.

He gasped and fought for breath. Then he emptied his glass slowly. This was something unbelievable—a liqueur in a million.

'I have judged,' he announced with due solemnity. 'But I have no words.'

'Yes. That is customary,' the proprietor replied courteously. 'I am glad you appreciate it. You will permit that I refill your glass?'

'Naturally.'

The proprietor did so.

'When one has had a murder in one's woodshed,' he said quietly, 'A drink of this quality can be of great help.'

M. Pinaud stared in astonishment.

'You know that too?'

'Of course. I told you that this is a small place. I will leave you the bottle to enjoy your drink. Let me know if there is anything else you require.'

And he went back to behind the bar.

M. Pinaud poured himself another cup of coffee. Then he drank a little slowly and lit a cigarette. The scalding hot liquid chased the liqueur down his alimentary canal, caught up with it, warmed and diffused it, until it seemed that his whole inside was nothing but one gigantic and comforting glow. It was a remarkable and unique sensation.

He sipped a little more of the liqueur and then began to think.

For years he had always thought that retirement would be a peaceful time. In the autumn of his life a man should be entitled to have both the time and the opportunity to occupy himself with all of those small but important and enjoyable tasks and hobbies a crowded, difficult and dangerous life had never permitted.

How wrong could one be.

Now, in its very inception, his retirement had become a mockery. Now he had very little money left. His wife's legacy had been expended on the house, which they both loved and would not dream of selling so soon. His only asset was a worn-out car. And he was suspected of murder by an idiot inspector.

If ever there was an occasion that called for a drink—then this was it.

He had another one. The coffee in his cup was by now not so hot, and therefore its resultant effect on his intestines not quite so remarkable as before.

He remedied this by pouring out a fresh cup from the coffee-pot and enjoyed a brief moment of complacency reflecting that his memory was still reliable and that he had not been the victim of his over-active imagination.

Obviously he had problems. He would have to face them with the same courage and determination that he had found in his more difficult and dangerous cases. He would have to give of himself, to the best of his ability, to the utmost of his strength. And then he would be helped, as he had so often been helped before . . .

He eyed his empty glass sternly.

You have a brain, Pinaud, he admonished himself severely. Use it. Think. Reason. Plan. Exercise your intelligence. Every problem has a solution. Find some for yours.

And since this bottle, so thoughtfully and considerately left here by this prince amongst proprietors, undoubtedly contains a stimulant such as you have never experienced before, it would seem only logical to have another drink to arouse and lubricate your cogitations.

Now whether this was wishful thinking on his part is a debatable point and a matter of conjecture, but nevertheless it is a certain fact that in a very short while (and three glasses later) he had an idea.

He had spent some of the time in recapitulating, almost word for word, his conversation with Inspector Javel. He remembered what had been said regarding Armand Brissac, the local jeweller. And here, without any further thought, was the solution.

As are so many solutions to insoluble problems, it was a simple one.

He would call to see Brissac and ask whether he could try to sell some of these gold rings the jeweller spent so much time in making. He would travel as an independent agent, pay his own expenses, and try to earn a commission.

In this way he could use his car once it had been

repaired, and turn the blue-suited *Sûreté* tycoon's somewhat dubious gift into a valuable asset. The car might be worn-out, but he would not be going far. Only to the local towns. He would be able to come back home for meals. He need not go out every day. There would still be time for all the work to be done in the sheds and the garden.

It seemed so simple that it was obviously the ideal solution. All great ideas, he reflected modestly, must fundamentally have a basic simplicity. Or else they would not work. In the resultant complacent mood of self-satisfaction at having thought of it, he reached out again for the bottle to celebrate.

Warmed and comforted by this truly remarkable distillation, he continued to think.

Over the years he had managed to amass an astonishing amount of information about a great number of things, but he realized now, in swift dismay, that he really knew very little about the art of salesmanship.

There were certain basic principles, naturally, which were obvious to commonsense and intelligence, but he had heard that there were schools and courses specially established to instruct in the art. What did they teach? He had no idea.

The basic principles were not difficult.

A salesman should obviously have good manners and be quietly yet if possible prosperously dressed, his linen immaculate and his finger-nails clean—if only not to disgrace both the prestige of the firm he represented and the owner of the shop while talking to him in the presence of customers.

There was also a psychological reason for this. An

owner or a buyer would inevitably wonder, even if it were subconsciously, whether he was missing something by not stocking these goods which apparently provided this traveller with such a good living. If he did not buy them, his competitors would.

A salesman should always be cheerful, even if business was bad and he was not feeling well nor happy, since cheerfulness is infectious. He should try to establish a personal relationship with his client by his sympathy and personality, so that if his name were ever mentioned at some trade conference or even in idle conversation, one of his clients might feel impelled to say: 'Oh yes, I do business with him. He has some good stuff—and he is such a nice man to deal with.'

And a salesman should never try to dominate the interview. His role should be that of a sympathetic listener. Most clients, being human, like to tell an audience how good they are at buying. This harmless idiosyncracy should be encouraged, never thwarted or interrupted.

A salesman should also know his trade and everything about the goods he is selling, conversant enough to answer any technical question competently and intelligently.

Here, at this juncture in his thoughts, M. Pinaud contemplated his empty glass gloomily. This one was going to be difficult. With all the rest he felt confident that he would be able to cope, but this one—what on earth did he know about gold rings?

The floorboards groaned. The whole building trembled. The proprietor appeared at his table, carrying a tray with a fresh pot of coffee.

'Forgive me for interrupting you, m'sieu,' he said cheerfully. 'You are obviously deep in thought. But this liqueur loses if the coffee with it is not scalding hot. I therefore took the liberty of making you a fresh pot.'

M. Pinaud looked up at him out of his dreams and visions and smiled, and the hard brooding lines of his features were transformed.

'Thank you,' he said quietly. 'You are a man after my own heart. I have been able to verify for myself the truth of your statement. And you are quite right. I have problems. That is why I am deep in thought and let the coffee get cold.'

The proprietor changed the coffee-pots.

'I do hope they are not because of your murder,' he said politely.

'Well, yes—in a way. And I have others as well. But may I remind you, m'sieu, that it is not my murder. It just happened to take place in my woodshed.'

'Of course. But to everyone here it is and always will be your murder. By some that is considered quite a distinction.'

'Indeed?'

'Oh yes. Indubitably. This Vervion is a quiet and peaceful place. It is buried in the heart of the country. Very little of note happens here. To have a murder on your doorstep—excuse me, on our doorstep—is something no-one is ever going to forget.'

'I am trying hard to see what you mean,' M. Pinaud told him patiently. 'You will forgive me if I add that I find it difficult to believe.'

The cheerful smile remained.

'No-one expects you to. You come from the big city,

where there is, naturally, an entirely different mentality. In a few years, with enthusiasm and application, you might be able to understand.'

'Now I do see what you mean. As I intend to live here for the rest of my life, I shall do my best to learn.'

'Good. You have the right spirit. That is more than half the battle. I wish you joy and good fortune, m'sieu.'

And the proprietor left him, carrying the cold coffee-pot.

M. Pinaud returned to his thoughts. He glanced at his watch. It would be better to wait until Monday to see the jeweller Brissac. Saturday afternoon was probably his busy time. He hoped that he would like and admire the rings when he saw them. A salesman had to be enthusiastic about the goods he offered—otherwise how could he hope to sell them? This was another one of the basic principles.

He drank more liqueur and more hot coffee. Suddenly, surprisingly, as an aftermath to so much intensive thinking, he felt not the mental exhaustion one would have expected, but an almost physical exhilaration.

There was no reason why he should not succeed.

He looked at the bottle. There was no point in leaving that ridiculously small amount which barely covered the bottom. The proprietor would charge him for it just the same.

The coffee was still hot. He emptied the bottle into his cup.

He, who had never been a salesman before, would do his best. No man could do more. There was too much at stake for him to fail. He would be all things to all men.

The fact that he knew nothing about what he was going to sell he would face, fairly and honestly, when it came up for discussion. Then he would tell the truth, and hope for consideration and understanding.

After all, truth had its own power, honesty its own impact. He could not envisage how being truthful and honest could possibly have an adverse effect on his sales.

He must remember to ask the proprietor if he would sell him another bottle of that remarkable liqueur, to set beside his bottles of absinthe. No household should be without one.

He went home to eat, and during the meal repeated to his wife most of the conversation he had had with Inspector Javel.

He was both eloquent (which was hardly surprising) and amusing in his descriptions of all the local suspects and spoke quite unconsciously with compassion about the dead girl, since in some indefinable way the inspector's condemnation of her character had only succeeded in arousing his pity, sympathy and understanding. And a smouldering and yet still savage anger at the man who had killed her.

But the fact that he himself was on the list of suspects he did not mention. This was unusual and out of character—indeed, the first occasion in a lifetime shared together on which he had not been utterly and completely truthful and frank. Their marriage had been too intensely happy and joyful to leave room for secrets, but now he felt, suddenly and strongly, that

Germaine had already had enough hard work and worry with the move and his unexpected retirement without giving her this further anxiety.

So instead he told her about his idea of trying to sell some of Brassac's rings on commission, and they discussed the project of his becoming a travelling salesman at some length and with considerable animation.

It was Germaine, with typically feminine logic, who made him realize a point he had completely ignored in his enthusiasm at his own ingenuity.

'But if the inspector told you that this Brissac is also one of his suspects—and if he should be the one—then how can he pay you for what you sell if he is arrested?'

He stared at her in dismay.

'I never thought of that.'

Then he took another mouthful of the exquisite local cream cheese and finished his glass of wine. Then he smiled at his wife. It was comforting to reflect on how so many problems seemed to shrink to insignificant proportions when viewed through the bottom of an empty wine-glass.

'Well—that could be,' he told her thoughtfully. 'But at the moment apparently there is no proof against anyone. And there are several other suspects. He is not the only one. It may be quite a time before the inspector has finished questioning them all, trying to find his proof.

'At least I can make a start. I shall see what happens. If I have any luck I could even perhaps get a bank loan or borrow some money to buy his stock if he should be the guilty one.'

He refilled his glass cheerfully. It was an excellent white wine, also purchased locally, dry, almost astringent, and even slightly *pétillant*—just the right thing after his somewhat complicated interview with the inspector and his session in the *café*.

'Now then. I will go to see him on Monday morning. There is really not much point in discussing the matter now—I do not even know if he will agree. So I have the week-end to help you. What is the most urgent job?'

'You said you had to do the woodshed—'

'No—no. That can wait. I could not face going in there now—I can still see her body in that case—'

'Of course. Let me think. There is really no hurry until the autumn. That will be the busy time. There will be several bushes to transplant—they are too big for me. All the apples to pick and store and the roses to prune. The gutters will need cleaning out soon. The house-martins started building their nests under the eaves the day the builders finished—their only nuisance was the mud they dropped on the front doorstep—but now the sparrows have come to do the same thing but under the pantiles and they are making a dreadful mess. But that too can wait.

'I know—the grass needs cutting badly. I would have done it myself last week, but I could not get that old machine to start. And I have so much planting and weeding—'

'Right. You get on with your weeding—it is a lovely evening to be outside. Make the most of it. I will wash-up for you and then cut the grass.'

He washed-up quickly, without chipping any of the

plates or breaking a glass—which was really a notable achievement if indeed somewhat surprising.

Then he read the instruction manual on the aged motor-mower he had bought from the previous owner. After which he changed into an old pair of trousers and went to wheel it out from the shed.

It was an incredibly ancient and remarkably heavy machine, standing massively on four rubber-tyred wheels, with a vintage Anzani engine and no box to collect the cut grass. Which meant the extra labour of raking after each mowing.

He checked the level of the oil and petrol, opened the petrol-tap, adjusted the carburettor control, grasped the handle of the starting-cord firmly and pulled, as advised in the manual, shortly, strongly and rapidly.

The engine turned, but did not fire. He pulled again. Nothing happened. He went on pulling until he was compelled to pause for lack of breath.

Then he went into the shed where he kept his tools and came back with various spanners. He knelt down, disconnected the lead and removed the sparking-plug. It was filthy, so encrusted with carbon that the gap was non-existent.

There was no need to buy a new one. In any case he had never had the time. This one would function if it were clean.

He sighed philosophically and went back into the shed for a penknife, sandpaper, a clean rag and a tin of petrol.

By the time he had finished cleaning the plug to his satisfaction, the petrol flooding the carburettor as a result of his frenzied pulling had evaporated, and at the first pull the engine fired healthily, raced and roared, and then settled down to a comforting if noisy rhythm as he adjusted the throttle.

He cleared up everything, rolled back his sleeves, and began to push the massive weight.

Then he looked ahead at the four large lawns, three of which were complicated fantastically by odd trees, bushes and flower-beds. He thought of the gutters to clean and the woodshed with all its logs to split, the apple picking and the transplanting in the autumn, the painting of fenceposts and the cementing of paths they had told the builders to leave, since by then their money was running out on the house alone, and he wondered somewhat gloomily how he would ever find time to sell any of Brissac's rings . . .

Which, as his chronicler (who is only concerned with the truth) is at pains to point out—even if any reader should be unkind and intolerant enough to think of such hurtful words as alcoholic depression—seems to him to be in the circumstances an entirely logical, understandable and characteristic thought . . .

FIVE

'But this is an extremely good clock,' said M. Pinaud.

'Correction,' replied Armand Brissac politely. 'This was once an extremely good clock. But now, I am afraid, it is a clock whose pivots are all completely worn-out. You have had it a very long time.'

He looked up from the alarm-clock he held in his large and capable hands and surveyed M. Pinaud with sympathy and understanding in his soft brown eyes.

M. Pinaud sighed and wondered how the years could have gone so quickly.

Then he looked at the man with interest. Brissac was tall and powerfully built, and wore an old but beautifully cut suit. In his expression there was both friendliness and compassion, but no trace of condescension, pity or contempt. By his voice and accent he had been to a very good school.

Then he smiled and held out his hand for the clock.

'Then you do not advise me to have it repaired?' he asked.

M. Pinaud's smile was infectious. A fine network of lines and wrinkles appeared at the corners of his eyes and the hard brooding strength of his features was transfigured.

Brissac smiled as well. Most people did.

'It would be a waste, M'sieu Pinaud, of both my time and your money. And then it would not be satisfactory. Far better to buy a new one. A clock of this type is not made to go for a very long time.'

'You know my name?' M. Pinaud asked with surprise. 'I have not been in here before.'

'Here in Vervion we all know everyone in it.'

'So I am given to understand.'

'I am sorry about the clock. Would you like me to—'

'No—no—that does not matter. It was only an excuse to come to see you.'

'Indeed?'

'Yes. I have heard that you make some very beautiful rings. And that you neither display nor sell them. Now I have a proposition, M'sieu Brissac. Would you be interested in allowing me to take some samples to the various jewellers in the towns around here and try to sell them for you on commission?'

Brissac considered thoughtfully, stroking his chin with one hand. Then he spoke.

'At first thought—yes. But why only the local towns? Why not Paris? My rings, I can assure you, are good enough for the *Rue de la Paix*.'

'I am sure they are. But my car is extremely old—something like my clock here. I would prefer for the moment to make shorter journeys in it. Paris is too far.'

'I see what you mean. Well—that might be a proposition of considerable interest,' Brissac said slowly.

'It would be for me,' M. Pinaud told him quietly. 'There is no question of might be.'
'And why is that?'
'Because I need the money.'
'Don't we all—in these days of inflation? I had occasion myself, quite recently, to need a fairly large sum in a hurry, which I was unable to find. I seem to have tied up all mine in buying gold to make my rings. I make them because I enjoy making them. But I am too busy to sell them.'

He paused for a moment. M. Pinaud waited politely for him to continue.

'I am a jeweller, M'sieu Pinaud, a goldmsith, a clock-repairer and a watchmaker. In this place there is no sale for jewellery, so I have to undertake clock and watch repairs to pay the rates and keep this incredibly ancient building from falling to pieces around me. Which leaves me with very little time for anything else.'

'And yet you find time to make rings?'
'I find time by making people wait for their repairs. There is no competition here for those. I make time because it is upon me to create. And I do not wish to lose my skill through lack of practice.'

He drew himself up and a note of pride rang in his voice as he continued:

'I make rings in the way my father taught me. I cast the gold on a charcoal in a hearthstone, overweight, in one long strip. Then I bend it round, cut it, solder the two ends together, and hammer on a triblet. Then I file the shank and the facets to the required design and weight. Each one is individual. No two rings are the

same. Would you care to see some?'
'I would—very much.'
'Then excuse me for one moment.'
He went out through an open door into an adjoining room, which had been fitted with a watchmaker's bench facing the window let into the wall.

M. Pinaud looked around him with interest.

The shop had once been the front room of that gracious house, but now its builders would never have recognized it.

A partition shut off the large bow window, in which were displayed watch-straps, alarm-clocks and some cheap silver jewellery. A similar selection was inside the glass-topped counter which divided the room in half. Two small benches stood in front of the counter, on which lay open a large repair-book with numbered pages and perforated and divided sections for tearing out as receipts. On the walls were clocks of all shapes and sizes, mainly cheap wall-clocks, amongst which several very fine bracket-clocks stood out incongruously.

Brissac came back with a small flat case in his hand. He opened it on the counter.

The gold signet-rings inside were beautiful. M. Pinaud picked one up and was surprised at its massive weight and grace.

'These are beautiful—really beautiful, M'sieu Brissac,' he said. 'I am sure I could sell some of them.'

Brissac looked at him thoughtfully for quite a while before answering. When he spoke M. Pinaud was surprised for the second time.

'Well—that is half the battle already won. I tell you

what—you have a try. You pay your own expenses and I will give you ten per cent commission on your sales. Give me a day to put price-tickets on them and make you up a varied selection—I have some more in the safe.'

He paused for a moment to reflect.

'You will need some business-cards and a duplicate invoice-book. I can find you those. You can use this case to show them. It is quite a good one. Come back to-morrow, M'sieu Pinaud, and I will have everything ready for you.'

M. Pinaud smiled again.

'Thank you very much. It is as simple as that? What about references? I can get you some.'

Brissac shook his head.

'There is no need for that. I shall ask you to sign a receipt for what you take, just as a formality, and for the sake of the insurance. But when someone owns a house like yours, references are hardly necessary. You can always sell it.'

Now it was M. Pinaud's turn to shake his head.

'That would break my wife's heart. But I would like you to know how much I appreciate your trust and confidence in me. I still find it strange that you know not only my name but even where I live.'

Brissac uttered a sudden barking laugh.

'I told you we all know everyone else's business here in Vervion,' he said. 'I know exactly what the builders have done to your house and I know all about your murder. I had that idiot Inspector Javel here this morning, trying to earn his salary by asking me a lot of stupid questions.'

'It is not my murder,' M. Pinaud told him patiently. 'It just happened to take place in my woodshed.'

'Which obviously makes it your murder. That is something you will have to accept. We were all sorry to hear about Louise. Everyone liked her. Completely without morals, of course—but a very charming person and a great character.'

He paused for a moment and sighed.

'I knew her well. I shall always remember how she came here once with her alarm-clock. She wanted it repaired and she wanted it in a hurry and this was clearly and obviously the most important repair of the year. She expected me to stop all my other work and attend to her personally without delay—so that her clock could wake her up at intervals during the night in order to copulate—she considered that it was a pity to waste valuable time in the unexciting pursuit of sleep.

'Without agreeing either with her principles or her perhaps distorted sense of values, it was impossible not to admire such enthusiastic and dedicated single-mindedness.'

'She seems to have been quite a person,' M. Pinaud said.

'She was that,' Brissac agreed. 'It is a pity, but such people bring trouble wherever they go.'

For a moment there was silence. M. Pinaud closed his eyes.

It was really astonishing how the image of Louise Voisin immediately appeared before them—her vitality and her laughter, her joyous acceptance of life, her whole-hearted enthusiasm, her demanding urgency, her obvious willingness to share it and her complete and unreserved agreement with all that this might entail . . .

Strange that he had not noticed all this when she had called to see them at their new house. Strange that he should think of it only now that she was dead.

But in the company of one's wife, he reflected philosophically, with all the experience born of a long marriage, perhaps—and perhaps not so much reasonably as certainly and necessarily—certain basic impulsions, although inevitable, were inexorably and rightly controlled. In these circumstances a wise husband kept his mouth tightly shut. And why not? Germaine had talked to Louise Voisin—not he. What on earth did he know about new heads for brooms, detergents and washing-up liquids?

All these thoughts had only taken seconds. He opened his eyes.

Brissac shut the case on the counter.

'Very well, then, M'sieu Pinaud. I shall expect you to-morrow.'

M. Pinaud thanked him once again with great sincerity and left the shop.

His car was on the hoist, looking strangely and pathetically naked and defenceless. Dufour's hands were filthy, his clean white coat stained with grease and oil, but his smile was as cheerful as ever.

Outside the wide open doors of the workshed, the builders were mixing and laying cement, not with any urgency or even appearance of haste, but with a philosophical acceptance of the indisputable fact that there were only so many hours in the day and a certain number of them had—mercifully—already passed . . .

'Well, m'sieu—I was right,' Dufour told him as he appeared. 'Mind you, I am not often wrong about these things, but I take no credit for that. After all, it is my trade, and it is not a good feeling for a man who takes a pride in his work to feel that he has made a mistake.

'The crown wheel in the differential and three bearings, two in the near rear-wheel and one in the off. The fitting is nothing. The dismantling has been a long job.'

He walked over to a low bench by the wall, picked up a clean rag and began to wipe his hands.

'I am very much obliged to you—'

'Not at all,' Dufour interrupted politely. 'It is for this that I am paid. I have only one obligation—to do the work well and earn my money honestly.'

M. Pinaud glanced pointedly at the lethargic builders.

'It is a great pity that more people these days do not think in the same way as you do,' he said.

'Maybe you are right. But I was brought up strictly by an old-fashioned father. I believe that many children around here to-day do not see very much of their parents. Which is a bad thing. Well—you should not have this trouble again, but you must realize and accept the fact that after such distances there has been a considerable amount of wear—'

'Everywhere else?'

'Exactly.'

'I see what you mean. Yes, this is only to be expected.'

'Mind you—if you continue to look after the car in

the way you have obviously been doing, and come to me as soon as you suspect that there is something wrong, there is no reason why you should not go on driving it for many years to come.

'You see, M'sieu Pinaud, it is not the age of a car which determines its performance, provided that it has been well made, but the way in which it has been treated and maintained. These factors have a greater influence on wear than the distance it has run.

'The man from whom you bought your house, M'sieu Douville, had one of the best models De Dion Bouton ever made. I should think it was probably as old as you are. I looked after it for him ever since I left school to help my father here. But all he ever did was to drive it to the Bank in the High Street and to The Seven Sons of Aymon twice a week, once every Sunday morning to church, and once a year to the coast, to Mouviers, for his holiday, which he spent fishing. The result is that it will take another fifty years for anything to wear out on that car. I hope he finds a garage to look after it well for him.'

He looked up at the dial-clock on the wall of the shed with dismay.

'But here I am wasting time talking—and time is the one thing of which there is never enough. I am afraid your car will not be ready until to-morrow evening, M'sieu Pinaud. I did not work yesterday. The Sunday before I had an urgent job which kept me here all day, and my wife was so upset she went off in disgust to see her mother. She has done that once a week ever since we were married, but never before on a Sunday. Having established a precedent, she did it again. So yesterday I did nothing, except housework. A man must eat. Therefore I am behind with my work.'

'That is quite all right,' M. Pinaud told him. 'I am in no violent hurry. The main thing is to make a good job of it, and I know you will do that.'

'You need have no worries on that account, M'sieu Pinaud. I was brought up in the old-fashioned tradition that there is only one way to do a job of work, and that is to do it well. But I do not like wasting time. Which I had to do this morning when that stupid arse Inspector Javel came here to interrupt this work and question me. Otherwise I would have been well ahead with your car and I could have finished sooner. But I had to waste valuable time answering his stupid questions about your murder.'

'It was not my murder,' M. Pinaud told him, with what was by now commendable self-control. 'It just happened that she was killed in my woodshed.'

'Well—if that does not make it your murder, then I am an unemployed bricklayer.'

M. Pinaud sighed. He began to realize that in the opinions of the inhabitants of Vervion this was and always would be his murder, and there seemed little to be gained by trying to deny the fact or even by arguing about it.

He looked at Dufour thoughtfully.

'I have heard two opinions of Inspector Javel this morning,' he said quietly. 'One was that he is an idiot, and now you refer to him as a stupid arse. These were not my impressions when I saw him. On the contrary, he struck me as being an extremely capable and intelligent man.'

Dufour laughed.

'He is,' he replied calmly. 'And a very ambitious one too. He is determind to get out of what he considers to be this primitive backyard into a position worthy of his manifold talents. It is that officious manner of his which upsets people.'

'Yes. That could be.'

'I did not really mind all his questions as to what I was doing last Sunday week. I suppose he is paid to ask them. It was his nasty insinuating manner that upset me. I told him what I told you—the truth. I was working here all day on an urgent job. And even if I had not been—would I be fool enough to tell him?'

'Hardly. For your information, M'sieu Dufour, I myself am on his list of suspects—'

'He must be mad.'

'Not necessarily. He is thinking logically. But he has no evidence. That is why I am going to try to clear myself as soon as possible by finding out who really did this brutal thing. I am determined to do so. After all, I have had some small experience with the *Sûreté*.'

Dufour stared in astonishment.

'The *Sûrete*? Then—then you are the famous Pinaud—'

'Perhaps I was once. Now I do not know what I am.'

'But we have heard and read about your exploits for years—even here in what Javel calls this primitive backyard.'

'For that you must thank my faithful chronicler,' said M. Pinaud modestly. 'He has worked hard and well.'

'But no-one has heard of your chronicler. Everyone knows about you.'

M. Pinaud sighed. He was fond of his chronicler and sometimes he found injustice depressing.

'You may be right.'

'Well—I find all this most interesting,' Dufour told him. 'I wish you luck in your investigations.'

'Thank you.'

'We were all sorry to hear about Louise. What a personality. What a character. She would drive up here in that small car she used to visit her clients, usually when I was madly busy, open the door wide and make such a performance of getting out in her short tight summer frock as to leave me in no doubt that she wore absolutely nothing underneath it.

'I am a very busy man, as you can see, and always what she wanted was some stupid little thing that she could easily have done herself. Every time she bought petrol there was the same routine.

'But she was so happy about it all—she enjoyed the act as much as the audience—that it was impossible to get annoyed with her.'

It might not have been wrong—it might even have been natural—to laugh at this recital. But M. Pinaud did not feel like laughing. The memories in his woodshed were too vivid, too poignant. He felt sad and bitter and confused.

As each man remembered and spoke about the dead girl, it was as if she became alive once again in the striking intensity of his vivid imagination—alive and compelling, happy and joyous, vital and vivid and carefree . . .

Gone to her Death 91

He sighed once again at the pity and the tragedy, the waste and the futility of it all . . .

With a start he realized that Dufour had been speaking.

'—get back to it now if I want to finish by to-morrow evening.'

'Of course,' he agreed at once. 'And I am sorry if I have delayed you by my talking. I will call in to-morrow evening to collect the car. Until then good-bye, M'sieu Dufour, and thank you very much.'

He walked away very slowly, his mind preoccupied with thought.

This Dufour was one of Inspector Javel's suspects. His money, or more probably his wife's money, was tied up with builders' invoices in the expansion of his garage. Any blackmailing demand for money would be more than he could face.

And the Sunday before last, the Sunday on which Louise Voisin had probably been killed, he could easily have left the car he was working on high up on the hoist, with all his tools spread out on the concrete floor of the shed, after Louise had seen the doors open and called on him.

The whole town knew that his wife invariably went to church every Sunday morning. Dufour could have asked Louise to take a walk through the copse to the garden. In Vervion no shed was ever locked. He could have explained so easily to the owner of the car that the repair had taken him longer than he had anticipated.

Even if Dufour had a grown-up son at an engineering college, what was his sex-life—with a wife who visited her mother so often? This was surely not natural. A daughter should have respect and loyalty and even devotion for her mother—yes—but her first duty was surely to her husband himself.

This was a pasture into which Louise Voisin would have been delighted to stray . . .

He was still trying to think it all out when he found himself outside the general clothing store of Macon & Son.

The shop had once been an imposing three-storey detached house. Now the two large bow-windows on either side of the vast doorway were filled with an astonishing variety of articles, from shirts, handkerchiefs and underclothes to boots, shoes, slippers, suits and raincoats.

M. Pinaud noticed that owing to its position on the rising land one could see his own house and part of his garden from any of the upper front windows.

Robert Macon was tall and thin. He wore a violent red check shirt, patched blue jeans and crêpe-soled boots. His hair was cropped short, his mouth was wide, wet, loose-lipped and lascivious. His features were redeemed by his deep-set intelligent eyes and a high and intellectual forehead.

'Good morning, M'sieu Pinaud. What can I do for you?'

'Good morning to you. You know my name?'

'Of course. Although we have not greeted you yet as a client.'

'I have been too busy moving into our new house. That will come later. Tell me—has Inspector Javel

been to see you?'
'No. Why should he?'
'You have heard about Louise—'
'Oh—that. Your murder?'
M. Pinaud sighed. There was no point in arguing any longer. To the inhabitants of Vervion it was now and always would be his murder. Still, he felt that he ought to make one last effort, if only because the completely unfounded and yet continually sustained implication was beginning to get on his nerves.
'Louise Voisin was murdered in my woodshed—yes.'
'Well—what on earth has that got to with me?'
M. Pinaud thought swiftly. It was hardly his place to tell this arrogant young man that he was one of the principal suspects. For that, Inspector Javel was paid his salary. He began to answer carefully, choosing his words with care.
'Apparently he is interviewing most of the men she knew intimately—'
Here he was interrupted by Macon's short sharp laugh.
'Then the poor fellow has got about six months' hard labour in front of him. It will take time for him to get around to me.'
He paused, and the deep-set eyes appraised M. Pinaud thoughtfully as he continued to speak.
'Mind you, this does not worry me. I have nothing to hide from him. Everyone knows that we were childhood sweethearts. I am not ashamed if they do know. On the contrary, I am proud of my memories. I have the most precious ones of all—the early ones—when

one first begins to explore the wonders and the delights of the female body. These I shall never forget.'

Again he paused. M. Pinaud did not speak. Then Macon's mood changed and once again he uttered that short sharp laugh.

'Of course, I have been accused by all the old washerwomen and busybodies in this place of being the only one responsible for starting her off on the downward path of sin, or corrupting a minor, of deflowering a virgin and fornicating with a child—and everything else you can think of. Absolute cock and nonsense. I can assure you, M'sieu Pinaud, that it was she who taught me—even at that age—all I know.

'She was a unique person—completely uninhibited—quite shameless. She enjoyed sex like some people enjoy eating and drinking. If it had not been with me at that time her first amatory explorations would have been with another. She was such a lovely person—such wonderful company. There were no hard feelings when she decided to enjoy her fun and games with someone else.

'Mercifully, I grew up. Which was something her very nature would never allow her to do, and during the process I realized—unlike her—that there were other and perhaps more worthwhile occupations than copulation.'

He finished, and the silence seemed to surge between them unendingly. Then M. Pinaud turned to go.

'I see. Thank you for your information, M'sieu Macon—although I am afraid it has not helped me very much.'

'Did you expect it to?'

'I had hoped—'
'Why?'
'Because I am going to find out who killed her.'

He spoke with a confidence and a conviction all the more compelling in that they were completely unconscious.

Something, in some indefinable way, seemed to change in Macon's manner.

'Indeed?'

'Yes.'

M. Pinaud's voice was expressionless, his features inscrutable.

'Shall we say that—since it was my woodshed—I have a personal interest in the matter?'

Macon did not reply.

'One more thing. It is fairly certain that she was murdered last Sunday week. I was not at home, and my wife went to church for the morning service. I notice that from the front windows here one can see my house. Did you see Louise Voisin or anyone else in the garden on that day?'

There was no hesitation in Macon's reply.

'No. I did not. My father and mother went to the sea for a drive. I was in my office at the back of the house for most of the day. I have plans for the expansion of this business which call for many hours of hard work.'

'I see. Well—thank you for your frankness. If your time is valuable, then I must not waste any more of it. Good-bye for now, M'sieu Macon.'

It was time he went home.

SIX

Two days later M. Pinaud drove into the outskirts of Locroix.

The morning before he had collected his samples, all neatly ticketed and priced, from Brissac. The ring case and duplicate invoice-book lay on the seat beside him.

The rest of that day had been exhausting. He had spent it climbing up and down the medieval tree-branch ladder which led from an upper back bedroom to the loft, storing all the boxes and cartons of disused possessions they had accumulated over the years of their married life.

There were the boxes of letters they had written to each other during their engagement and when he had been away on long cases, there were photo-frames and picture-frames, pieces of linoleum and carpet which might have been useful for repair, curtains which might have fitted in the new house but did not, together with their rails, slides and hooks, childhood books and comics belonging to the children—and many other things he had promised himself to sort out when he retired. And now there was barely time to stack them away neatly where they would not be seen.

Gone to her Death 97

In the morning he had collected his car. Dufour's diagnosis had been correct, his workmanship exemplary. The maddening noise had now completely disappeared. It was impossible not to feel cheerful and optimistic.

He had made an early start, and yet even so the streets of this fairly populous and prosperous town seemed strangely deserted.

He saw a large policeman standing impassively beside the next traffic-lights, made up his mind suddenly, braked and swung the car in towards the pavement just as the lights changed to red.

He lowered his window and addressed the man politely.

'Excuse me, Officer—I am a stranger in this town. Could you tell me where I can find the principal jewellers here?'

From beneath the wide, virile and luxuriant moustache there piped, in amazing incongruity, a high falsetto voice.

'Why—yes, m'sieu. Follow this road to the next traffic-lights, which is where the two main shopping streets intersect. They are all near each other, grouped around those cross-roads.'

'Thank you very much. That will be useful. Is there a parking-place near?'

'Yes. Turn right at the lights. There is a sign.'

Calmly and purposefully he leaned forward and looked at the sample-case and invoice-book on the other seat.

'But you will not need it to-day, m'sieu,' he added.

'Why not? Surely it will be easier to walk, since all

the shops are near each other?'

'Because to-day is Wednesday.'

'I know that. What can—'

'And Wednesday is early-closing day here in Locroix. Hee-hee-hee.'

The falsetto laugh indicated that this individual considered such information, particularly to a stranger, to be highly amusing. It is hardly surprising to relate that M. Pinaud found some difficulty in agreeing with him. He stared at the man in dismay.

'But—but you said early-closing—surely it is early enough—'

'Hee-hee-hee. I am sorry, m'sieu, but here in Locroix it is an age-old custom that all the jewellers shut their shops throughout the day, to compensate for the fact that they remain open all day on Saturday. Only the food shops are open in the morning.'

'I see.'

He could not blame the man. It was his own fault. He should have checked such a thing for himself before leaving.

It was just that he was not at the moment in the right mood to listen to that irritating laugh. He was completely unable to find any vestige of humour in the situation. This work was too important to him, his disappointment—after the cheerful optimism with which he had left his house—too intense, to listen to this fatuous sniggering.

'How far to Montville?' he asked, shortly, savagely and sharply.

The laughter ceased abruptly, perhaps because of what was clearly apparent in his voice, or perhaps because the policeman had enjoyed his joke, but now even he realized that it was over.

'About forty kilometres, m'sieu. You will be all right there. Early-closing to-morrow.'

'Thank you.'

He raised the window, started the engine and waited for the lights to change. Then he drove on to Montville.

The man behind the counter was young, florid, aggressive and worried.

He made no attempt to conceal either his aggression or his worry as M. Pinaud opened the door of his shop and walked confidently inside.

It was perfectly obvious from his appearance that he had a problem on his mind, and that at this particular moment he needed company in his shop as much as he needed a hole in his head, and from his exasperated glance it was also apparent that his problem was important and complicated enough to include prospective clients in the category of unwelcome visitors—which, M. Pinaud thought swiftly, was both interesting and unusual, since the man's living—whatever his problems—undoubtedly depended only on people opening his front door.

Clad in his best suit, and with a slim black case under his arm, M. Pinaud could easily have been a successful and prosperous lawyer who had decided to marry his typist and was therefore about to purchase an expensive engagement ring to assure her of the respectability of his pre-conjugal sexual activities.

He put on his best smile and remembered the name of the shop, which he had carefully noted as he entered.

'Good morning to you. Are you M'sieu Bonnard?'

He had been told that it was always an excellent thing to personalize the meeting as soon as possible, and that it was an essential requisite to know the buyer's name before trying to sell him anything.

'No, I am not. Bonnard has been dead for more than a hundred and fifty years. My grandfather bought this shop and the name. I am Jules Mercier.'

'I see. Thank you. I did not know. This is the first time I have been here in Montville. My name is Pinaud. May I show you some very beautiful rings?'

'Normally the answer would be yes. To-day it is no. My wife is expecting a baby.'

'Ah—then—quite apart from congratulations—this is a very worrying time for you, M'sieu Mercier,' M. Pinaud said quickly. 'I am a father myself. I know '

Something in his voice, some almost indefinable nuance of understanding and sympathy, seemed to penetrate and destroy the man's aggressiveness. His voice was definitely more cordial as he replied.

'It is not that which is worrying me. She is quite capable of having a baby. To a woman it is a natural thing. For that she was created. What is driving me mad is the fact that they insist on me being there with her to hold her hand while she has it.'

M. Pinaud was surprised.

'But that is surely an extraordinary thing—'

'That is exactly what I think myself. Apparently this is the new modern idea, rooted in the latest concepts of psychology, to give the mother courage and to instil some of the basic responsibilities of parenthood into the father's thick head.'

Here he sighed profoundly.

'To drive home his guilt, I suppose. What would the psychiatrists think of that? It seems strange to me—but then I know that I am a simple man—that both my mother and my grandmother managed perfectly well to perpetuate the family without any such help.'

M. Pinaud could hardly believe his ears.

'But I would have thought that the last person a mother would wish to be there, apart from the doctor and the nurse, would be her husband. It is not an easy—'

'I know—I know. But now they have talked her into it. They say it is essential for both of us and for the future welfare of the child. I refused the doctor a dozen times. Now they have convinced her. They know, the cunning bastards, that she is the one person I am unable to refuse. I shall faint on the floor. I know I shall. I have dreamed about it for weeks.'

'Not necessarily,' M. Pinaud told him. 'When the actual time comes you will find the courage. Nothing is ever as bad as a vivid imagination can distort it.'

'Do you really think so?' Mercier asked, eagerly and hopefully.

'Definitely. I not only think so, but I know so. I have proved it myself, not once but countless times.'

For a moment there was silence, while Mercier looked at him thoughtfully.

'You are a very sympathetic man, M'sieu Pinaud,' he said slowly. 'And if I may say so, a very unusual traveller.'

M. Pinaud smiled.

'That is not surprising. This is my first day as a

traveller. And this is my first call.'

'Really? Well—as I said, I cannot possibly see you to-day. I am waiting now for the telephone-call. Come and see me later, when all this is over. Show me what you have to sell and tell me all about it.'

'Thank you, M'sieu Mercier. I will do that. Good-bye for now. And my best wishes to you both—and *bon courage*.'

As they shook hands he noticed that for the first time since he had entered the shop, Mercier was smiling.

In the next shop an exquisitely dressed and very urbane gentleman greeted him with pity, condescension and barely concealed disdain.

He listened courteously enough to what M. Pinaud had to say.

'Of course. Show me what you have. I would be failing in my duty to my superior and to my fellow directors if I did not consider everything new offered to me.'

M. Pinaud could accept the condescension and even the disdain. It was one of the fundamental laws of economics that a buyer was automatically elevated, because of his status, to a far higher and more distinguished position than a seller, this being in no way a personal issue, but merely the inevitable result of the application of the economic forces of supply and demand.

But the pity rankled. He did not need, nor did he ask for pity. He was trying to earn his living fairly and honestly, and either he would sell his rings or he would not.

Inwardly he tensed and forced himself to concentrate on what he was doing. As he took out a ring from the case and offered it for inspection, he could not help wondering who this arrogant and self-righteous type would ever dream of acknowledging as his superior. It could well be the bank-manager who held his overdraft. The idle thought soothed his bitterness and he felt more cheerful.

The name above the shop had been Hector Masseron. His previous experience with names had made him somewhat uncertain, but it was unlikely that a second jeweller so near to the last would also have been dead for one hundred and fifty years.

'Do you like this one, M'sieu Masseron?' he asked politely.

Across the two lower pockets of this individual's brocaded and lapelled waistcoat hung a massive gold chain. Delicate fingers with manicured nails now pulled out a magnifying eye-glass attached to one end of the chain and Armand Brissac's workmanship was meticulously examined.

'Well, now—this is a very fine ring,' Masseron announced after a lengthy inspection. 'How much are you asking for it?'

'Please excuse me, m'sieu,' he replied. 'The price is on the ticket—I am afraid I have only just collected them.'

Inwardly he cursed himself for not having memorized the numbers and prices of the rings before he started out. This—one did not have to attend a salesmanship course to know—was not a good answer.

He was in competition with all the young and

aggressive types who chased across the country in their powerful company cars, parked on the pavement outside the jeweller's shop, bawled to any protesting policeman that their stock was worth millions of francs, and then proceeded to stagger with seven heavy cases through the doorway.

He knew. He had already seen them. They were the new generation—brash, competent, arrogant and unafraid. And on the ball. They knew all their prices by heart. They would never have asked a buyer to look at a ticket.

Mind you, he would have been prepared, as a matter of common courtesy, to examine the ticket himself to answer the question, but as the ring was in Masseron's hand and close to his eye, this was hardly possible.

'That is a very high figure.'

The voice was cold and discouraging. Perhaps the bitterness of his recent reflections were responsible—he did not know—but quite unconsciously his own as he replied was very similar, and it had a hardness in it as well.

'Yes. As you have just seen and confirmed, it is a very heavy, beautifully made and expensive ring.'

'I can buy a similar article from one of my regular suppliers for very much less.'

'The same weight?'

'Of course.'

'Indeed? Would you care to weigh this one?'

It was difficult, and perhaps hardly tactful, to call a prospective client a liar, but M. Pinaud felt, with some justification, that he had made his point and that the implication had been noted.

He had never considered the matter of prices before—there had been no occasion—but he was quite convinced that Brissac's expenses in Vervion compared very favourably with those of any established Parisian firm of ring-makers, and unless he had made a mistake, there was no reason why his prices should not be competitive.

Now, if this jeweller took a ring from his stock and weighed them both, to compare and to prove his contention, then obviously he would accept the evidence of the scales and apologize.

But Masseron did not do this. He allowed his eyeglass to drop from his eye and placed the ring carefully back in the case.

'That will not be necessary,' he said loftily. 'Holding the ring in the palm of my hand is quite enough. Over the years one tends to gain a certain expertise.'

'Naturally,' M. Pinaud agreed politely.

Masseron looked at several more rings and asked the prices, which M. Pinaud told him.

Then he stepped back, replaced the glass and the end of the chain in his waistcoat pocket and shook his head regretfully.

'No. I am sorry, M'sieu Pinaud—but I do not see any reason why I should buy any of these rings. You will appreciate, of course, that we have been doing business—a very large and profitable business—with certain well-established firms for many years, and without a very good reason it does not seem right to abandon or neglect those who have served us so well and faithfully in the past.'

M. Pinaud thought swiftly what he ought to say.

'I would have accepted the fact that these rings were more than a very good reason, M'sieu Masseron. And I am not asking you to abandon or neglect any of your suppliers—only to try one or two of them in addition to what you already have in stock, which will probably give you a chance of increasing your turnover.'

Even as he listened to his own words he knew that he was wasting his time. The man had no intention of buying. Then why on earth had he not said so honestly, instead of telling lies about prices and weights? Perhaps it was his own fault. He had been wrong to upset him. One should never argue with a buyer. Even he, with less than an hour's experience as a traveller, should have known that.

He watched Masseron continue to shake his head and knew that he hated him and would never call there again. He closed his case, said good-bye politely and left the shop.

This travelling business was definitely more difficult than it had seemed to him in *The Seven Sons of Aymon* . . .

There were only two more jewellers' shops in Montville.

The first one had its main window boarded with planks. Three white-overalled carpenters were busy in front of it with rulers, hammers, saws and chisels.

Inside an extremely worried and harassed individual listened to him with growing and ill-concealed impatience, which finally exploded in a torrent of words, into which he was obviously releasing all his pent-up anger, frustration and rage.

'Look—whoever you are—you ought to know better than to come in here worrying me at a time like this. You saw for yourself as you came in. Our window was smashed on Sunday night by some hooligans. I spent the whole of Monday morning on the telephone—no local firm would even board it up until I had confirmation from the insurance company. Those fools made me wait until this morning. I had to engage and pay a local carpenter to board it up on Monday afternoon, so that I could be sure the shop was safely shut at night.

'Now at last the firm they stipulated must be engaged have started—three men, mind you, not one, and they say it will take at least a week to put in a new window.

'I don't want to see anyone. I don't want to buy anything. All my time is spent in trying to explain to my customers why we shall be a whole week without a window display. Good-day to you, M'sieu Pinaud. Come and see me next month. Not now. I am busy.'

In the second shop a smartly dressed middle-aged lady was sitting on a large chair behind the counter. She listened attentively to what he had to say, studying him meanwhile with marked and obviously growing disapproval, and then reached up to smooth her very expensive and elaborate *bouffant* hair-style with one well-manicured hand.

She waited courteously enough until he had finished, and then began to speak, slowly and deliberately at first, but then in a rapidly increasing tempo, until to him the spate of words seemed to be literally pouring out in a torrent over his unprotected head.

'Oh no—I am afraid that would be impossible— quite impossible. M'sieu Oullens has an inflexible rule, from which he never deviates. I am his personal secretary and I ought to know. He never sees any representative of any firm without an appointment made in writing well in advance.'

She patted her head again.

'He is a very busy man. His interests, quite apart from this shop, are wide and varied. You will have to write, enclosing a business card, stating in detail the nature of your business, and give at least four or five factual reasons why you consider that the stocking of your merchandise would be to our mutual benefit.'

Once again she smoothed and patted her hair.

'I should also tell you that no appointment is ever made except on Friday, which is the one day M'sieu Oullens devotes wholly, in spite of the ramifications of all his other and varied interests, to the management of this shop. I would also think it remiss of me if I did not advise you to wait at least a month before you write, as our stock is extremely high and our buying, as is customary in this trade, is seasonal. And there is one other point of great importance.'

She continued to speak, but he was no longer listening. Her narrow features, with their long upper lip, reminded him forcibly of a well-bred horse. And her hand never stopped that maddening patting and smoothing of her hair.

He drew himself up to his full and impressive height and then bowed with an old-fashioned and courtly grace.

She stopped talking and stared at him in amazement. Travellers never bowed. The last man she had seen bowing had been her grandfather.

'Thank you, madame,' he said politely, 'For all your information and your help. Good-day to you.'

As he left the shop he thought that his life was already complicated enough without having to pander to the whims of the inflexible M. Oullens.

He decided to call it a day.

He drove back through Locroix and was not very far from Vervion when he noticed the excessive play in his steering-wheel.

He reduced his speed immediately and wondered what he should do. He was on the second-class road which ran through the rich farming countryside a few kilometres north of Vervion.

He could either abandon the car and wait for the first passing motorist to give him a lift to Dufour, or else continue, slowly and carefully—which would nevertheless save him a good deal of time—and hope that he would reach the garage before the trouble became worse.

The decision was made for him.

The road curved around the boundary of a cornfield. He turned the wheel and touched the brake with his foot. The car kept on in a straight line, towards the low grass bank and the irrigation ditch.

Instinctively, the touch became a powerful stamp on the brake-pedal, which locked the wheels. There was mud and manure on the road, scattered liberally from an overloaded farm trailer. The car skidded on it— gently, since his speed had not been great—but completely out of control, because it no longer responded to the steering.

The front wheels mounted the bank, dipped and dropped as the undershield ploughed into the soft earth, and then came to rest, hanging over the ditch.

Three hours later he stood beside a very contrite Dufour under the hoist in the garage at Vervion.

It had all taken a long time, because in that peaceful corner of the world passing motorists were rare while there was a mid-day meal to be eaten, and Dufour himself was in the habit of eating late and therefore needed more time to finish his own. And then the tow had been a difficult, awkward and lengthy process.

He had accompanied Dufour in the breakdown lorry, both to show him the scene of the accident and also to ensure that his beloved car did not suffer any further damage.

His thoughts were gloomy and bitter. All this would cost him more money, when he had not yet even received the bill for the last repair. And everyone else in the world seemed to have time to eat and enjoy lunch—except him. And his complete failure to earn any commission that morning did not help his despondency.

'I am very sorry that you should have had this trouble, m'sieu,' said Dufour as he shone the beam of a powerful hand-lamp upwards. 'But you must realize and remember that I had a major repair to do for you with the back axle and obviously I did not have time to check every component. Your steering was perfectly normal when I drove the car the other day. But as I said then, this car has had a lot of wear. Ah—there—I thought it would be that—'

He pointed to where the end of the steering-arm lay loosely across the track-rod.

'There was a nut there joining those two when the car was made, and a split-pin set through two holes in the end of the bolt for safety. But with time and wear and bad weather, and the resultant rust and corrosion, who can say what will happen to a split-pin, which is after all only a small and very thin piece of steel? There is no split-pin there now.

'It must have either worn out or sheared off against some flying stone or piece of metal flung up from the road some time recently, with the result that whenever the steering-wheel was turned a pressure was put on the nut, inducing it to loosen. To-day it finally came off.'

He switched off the lamp and walked out from under the hoist.

'It is a good thing you were going slowly, M'sieu Pinaud,' he said quietly. 'Or else you might have had a very bad accident.'

M. Pinaud looked at him thoughtfully. The man's eyes were expressionless.

'Yes,' he agreed slowly. He did not voice his thoughts, which, although confused, were mainly occupied with the three disturbing facts that—first, he had never heard of steel disintegrating without unlubricated friction, secondly, the chance of a flying stone or piece of metal striking that particular part was one in a million, and thirdly, that there could never have been a better opportunity to remove a split-pin and loosen a nut than when the car had been on this same hoist for a back axle repair . . .

'Yes,' he repeated. 'With a car like this, one would be expected to drive fast. Is there any other damage?'

'Nothing that can't be put right by this time to-morrow. The undershield and front bumper are bent. I can straighten those. You will need a new number-plate, new locking-nut and split-pin, and a test for wheel-alignment. I will have it ready for you this time to-morrow, M'sieu Pinaud.'

He was thanked politely.

'That is very kind of you, M'sieu Dufour. I would like to use the car again as soon as possible, and I appreciate your help. I will call for it to-morrow evening—that will be soon enough. Good-bye and thank you.'

He walked home very slowly, in spite of the fact that he was starving with hunger, absorbed by the complexity of his thoughts.

As Inspector Javel had said, there might be suspicion, but there was no evidence and no proof.

SEVEN

Dr. Poidevin was tall and handsome, with long and beautifully waved blond hair. His teeth were large and white and prominent when he smiled.

He smiled now, seated behind his large and imposing desk, and looked at the occupant of the patient's chair opposite with a shrewd and appraising glance.

'Well now, M'sieu Pinaud—what can I do for you? You look far too healthy to be a patient.'

'I am not a patient, Doctor Poidevin. I am glad and thankful to say that my health is exceptionally good.'

The smile faded.

'But—but these are surgery hours. You made an appointment—'

'I know I did. But you are a very busy man, and I wanted to see you as soon as possible about an entirely different matter. This seemed to me to be the best way to see you.'

'I have patients waiting in the surgery—'

'I shall not keep you longer than any one of them.'

'What is this matter?'

'I would like you to tell me something about Louise Voisin.'

At the mention of her name, it seemed to him that the man tensed, slightly but unmistakably, and yet the immediate self-control was so effective that it almost made him wonder if he had been mistaken.

'Why?'

M. Pinaud thought swiftly before he answered. This was a very cool and competent type, completely master of himself, and not likely to give anything away. And yet he was certain that the mention of the dead girl's name had both surprised and shaken him.

'Let us say that I consider I have a proprietary interest in her—in view of the fact that she was murdered in my woodshed.'

'That has nothing to do with you.'

'No. Particularly as I was not even here the Sunday before last, which I am told is probably the day on which she was killed. I was in Paris.'

'Then why—'

'Because that fact is not good enough for Inspector Javel. According to him, I could have driven out here in time to murder her, and get back quickly enough to establish an alibi there.'

'After having chosen the one place in the whole town to commit your crime which would be sure to involve and implicate you? I would not take any notice of that idiot if I were you, M'sieu Pinaud.'

'I thought the same—at first. But now I realize that the only way to clear myself of his suspicion is to find out who really did it. So I am asking various people certain questions about her, trying to build up an estimation of her character and what kind of person she really was. In this way I shall probably find some clue.'

'But I hardly knew her—'
'She was your patient.'
'Only recently. Only when she became pregnant.'
For a moment there was silence. M. Pinaud waited patiently. Dr. Poidevin contemplated his clean blotting-paper with such undivided concentration that M. Pinaud wondered what he was thinking.

Then the doctor raised his eyes frankly. They were blue and intense, and then remote as he remembered. As he spoke his voice was slow and thoughtful.

'Very well. There is nothing to distort, nothing to conceal. Louise Voisin was beautiful—not only in features and body, but in mind and spirit as well. She had a quality of grace and a zest for living which were so intense that it is almost impossible to describe them in words. And she was completely amoral and overwhelmingly fascinating.

'You can imagine the effect of all this on some of the characters here. Not on me, fortunately.'

Here, surprisingly, he looked up and smiled.

'I should think the explanation is simple enough. After all, I am—I hope—in no way abnormal. But doctors as a class must—by reason of the very nature of their profession—have different reactions. The human female body, because it is usually concealed and clothed attractively, and powdered and perfumed, is bound normally to be charming, provocative and enticing. But a doctor, who spends so much time in the continual clinical examination of it, must inevitably lose sight of most of that mystery and fascination which makes it so alluring. He therefore is forced to cultivate an impersonality in order to function efficiently as a doctor. Or perhaps this comes naturally as a mechanism of self-defence—I do not know.'

Again he paused, but this time he did not look up as he continued to speak. M. Pinaud had the strange impression that he was not being told anything directly, but that the doctor was reciting, in an even and controlled tone, something that he had previously taken the trouble to learn by heart.

'She knew all this. There was nothing that girl did not know about sex and men. She had been to see various other doctors in the locality before she came here to me—the usual minor anxieties and manifestations that usually accompany excessive sexual indulgence at an early age.

'Naturally I knew all about her long before she came. We doctors have a very close communal life in these country districts. There is not a lot that we do not know about our patients.

'But it was the zeal and the zest and the wholehearted enthusiasm with which she tried to break down this barrier between us, this impersonality I was talking about, that really and truly fascinated me. With her it became a point of honour—a challenge to her personal pride—to prove that even though I was a stuffy, strait-laced, narrow-minded and definitely repressed type, her lovely body would surely be provocative and desirable enough to arouse me from my impersonal and monastic torpor.'

The even voice ceased. M. Pinaud did not speak. The blue eyes looked up at him, seemed to refocus, and then became once more intense and compelling.

'She tried hard enough, M'sieu Pinaud. I give her

credit and full marks for that. But she did not succeed.'
Again he paused. Once more M. Pinaud waited. The silence seemed to surge between them, slow and sorry and sad—and laden with so many memories.

'And even if she had,' Dr. Poidevin said suddenly, but without any change at all in the even tone of his voice, 'You can be quite sure that I would not tell you. It is none of your confounded business.'

M. Pinaud stood up.

'I quite agree with you,' he said quietly. 'Try to remember that I did not ask you. One last question—when she consulted you about her pregnancy—did she ask you to—'

Dr. Poidevin remained seated. His finger had been on the bell-push button which would summon the next patient from the waiting-room, but he did not press it.

'No,' he interrupted. 'She did not. She obviously wanted to have the child. Even though a terminated pregnancy is not a complicated matter these days.'

M. Pinaud closed his eyes. He saw Louise Voisin again as he always saw her whenever these men described her—alive and not dead—vivid and real, gay and reckless, eager like a flame to consume and consummate that unending flow of spirit and energy which had made her so desirable, so lovely and so vulnerable . . .

Naturally, she would have wanted the child. Of course she would never have thought of destroying it.

He opened his eyes and shivered, and when he spoke his voice was soft and sad.

'That is why she was killed.'

Then he turned and left the doctor alone.

'I call it damned and confounded impertinence. I refuse to answer your questions, M'sieu Pinaud.'

The bull-like voice was in keeping with General Correvon's huge frame, bushy moustache and gleaming bald head. It was a voice, harsh and powerful, that in its life had caused colonels, majors and captains to jump to attention, lieutenants to wilt and even sergeants to blench. It was more than a voice—a rasping roar that filled the large and beautifully furnished room, into which he had been asked, with sound and quivering fury.

'I can tell you here and now that it is fortunate for you that you did not see my wife at the door, or else you would be outside by now. It was bad enough with that idiot Javel and his endless cross-examination when I thought I was doing the correct thing and my duty as a citizen by going to see him. I give orders, I would like you to know, M'sieu Pinaud. All my life I have given orders. I do not take them.'

The tremendous voice roared on and on. M. Pinaud neither wilted nor blenched, nor did he jump to attention. It was not easy. He had to remind himself that he was not in uniform.

He sat composedly in the comfortable chair to which the general had waved him imperiously, and smiled with sympathy and understanding. He had dealt with this type before. He could do so again. A young girl had been killed and he was suspected of the murder. Nothing else was as important. Nothing else mattered.

'I appreciate your courtesy in seeing me, General Correvon,' he said quietly. 'I am sure that these few questions will not—'

'You have no right to come in here and ask questions,' the great voice interrupted him, successfully drowning his quiet and even tones. 'You have no status.'

'I had a certain amount once. In the *Sûreté*.'

'I don't care a damn what you had once. Now you are just another stranger come to live in this town. There are far too many already. I would forbid it if I could. All these idiot farmers are selling good agricultural land because they get higher prices for building lots. The government must be mad to allow it. Soon the whole countryside will be covered with houses and factories, instead of growing food, and all the fools in this country will starve to death. Serve them right. The *Sûreté*—bah—what is that? Now if it had been the Army—'

'I was in that too.'

M. Pinaud felt that perhaps it was his turn to interrupt. The effect was remarkable. The hot and angry eyes stared at him fiercely and incredulously from under the tufted eyebrows.

'Where?'

'Not in your army, General. But it was the same war. Only we had no uniforms—no tanks or guns. We had to fight in the dark, with knives and plastic bombs and sticks of dynamite—'

'The Maquis—'

'Yes.'

The general looked at him with a new interest, even with respect. He actually made an effort to modulate his voice, but without success.

'No-one told me that,' he said.

'It was a long time ago.'

'To me it was yesterday.'

'That is because you live with your memories. I have no time for mine. There is always something new happening. Such as the murder of Louise Voisin.'

'Why should you want to know about her?'

'Because she was killed in my woodshed and therefore Inspector Javel thinks that makes me a suspect.'

'Rot. Cock. The man is a lunatic.'

'He is the law. He has—shall we say—status.'

The craggy lined features split—suddenly and charmingly—into an enormous grin.

'*Touché*,' he bellowed. Then he settled back in his own chair.

'What do you want to know?'

'Everything.'

'Why?'

'Because I am going to find out who killed her. It is the only way to clear myself of suspicion.'

'Then you are going to be unlucky. I know very little about her. Mind you—I liked her. I do not mind admitting it. We all liked her. In spite of the gossip and malicious lies you get from all the old frumps in a small place like this, there was nothing really wrong with the girl—all she needed was a father to put her over his knee and smack her bottom. That she never had.

'But what a damn fine soldier she would have made, had she been born a man. She knew her own mind. She knew exactly where she was going and what she was doing. And she had courage. She was prepared to pay the price—any price.'

He paused for a moment and sighed.

'But when she came round here trying to blackmail me, she picked the wrong man. That is what I told Javel. Excuse me.'

He heaved up his huge, gaunt and yet still powerful frame from the chair and went to the sideboard. He came back with a large bottle of brandy and two tumbler glasses.

He set them on the table in front of him and poured—with M. Pinaud watching him in unbelieving fascination—until the two large glasses were filled to the brim.

'M'sieu Pinaud,' the general pronounced with formal courtesy when he had finished, 'It is an honour for me to drink with one of the *Maquis*. Your very good health.'

It was a few seconds before M. Pinaud was able to control his voice sufficiently to reply. A sudden surge of emotion at the superb generosity of this gesture and tribute—from a man whose reputation as a fighting soldier had made history—brought a mist to his eyes.

'Thank you. And yours.'

They drank. Then M. Pinaud watched, incredulously, as the general tilted the tumbler, threw back his head and drained the glass as if he had been drinking beer.

'My wife,' he announced loudly when he had finished, 'Tells me that I am an irascible and cantankerous old bastard. Maybe she is right. I do not know. At my age I have come to believe that there is no such thing as an unreserved and unqualified judgement. I prefer to think that I am only a normal man, brought up to a certain standard of values, who is now compelled to watch their erosion and decay and total obliteration. This I find hard.'

He grasped the bottle with a fierce gesture and refilled his glass. M. Pinaud had sipped about a third of his. The brandy was strong, and yet exquisitely smooth and mature. He shook his head as the bottle was thrust at him. The general lifted his own glass and drank about half of its contents.

'At least I know my own mind. I have always known what I was doing—even when sending good men to die—and where I was going. Which is more than most people seem to do to-day.

'When I read my morning newspaper, M'sieu Pinaud, I do not mind telling you that I get thoroughly depressed. There is nothing in it but violence, murder and filth. And preparations for the next war. Surely the last one should have been a warning and a lesson for mankind. I ought to know. I gave six years of my life to fighting it, and watched the house in which my family had lived for nearly a thousand years—with my three sons in it—blown to pieces by land-mines. I think the whole world is going mad.

'Juvenile delinquency—old people being attacked and beaten up—what kind of homes do these thugs come from? How have their parents brought them up?

'If I had my way, because I believe that crime increases if the punishment lightens, I would shoot every fifth one arrested—just as an example. And the others I would flog until they were unconscious. They need to be exterminated—in the same way that one steps with a heavy boot to squash some poisonous bug. The shooting and the flogging should be given front-page publicity by law in all the newspapers, as priority over what they print to-day. That would make some of these thugs pause and reflect—those who were thinking of doing the same thing next week.

'We never had a crime problem in the army. The punishment was far too severe. What do they do now? Send these apes—these sub-men—to a reform school for a short time—because they are so young—so that they are worse when they come out.'

He emptied his glass with two huge gulps.

'I tell you, M'sieu Pinaud, that our so-called civilization is going to the dogs. Each nation needs a strong man at the top. Where are the strong men to-day? Where are they? You name them—if you can.'

He glared at M. Pinaud fiercely and accusingly, and then refilled their glasses with brandy, ignoring M. Pinaud's protestations that he had had enough.

M. Pinaud named one.

The hot and angry eyes seemed to glow with a new intensity.

'Yes—yes—no argument. You are right. You ought to know. But, mercifully, they have left him with only half a country. Which is a good thing, and sound commonsense, or else by now you and I would probably be fighting them all over again. And I am too old. I do not want to fight again.'

'I am not too old to fight for what I believe in,' M. Pinaud told him. 'But just now I am too busy. My life has become complicated, just when I thought that it would be peaceful. I have got to find the murderer of Louise Voisin.'

The general looked at him shrewdly and appraisingly. He was now delicately sipping his brandy with obvious enjoyment and appreciation after having swallowed the contents of two large glasses as if they had been beer.

'That you will never do,' he roared in his tremendous voice, with a gusto and a conviction that M. Pinaud found difficult to ignore. 'With anyone else in this place—yes. But not with her. She was unique. She was far too fond of having it stuck into her. Too many men could so easily have been responsible. But what a girl—what a glorious creature—what a soldier she would have made.'

Perhaps if he went to the woodshed and chopped up those two packing-cases into planks for firewood—perhaps then he would not think about her so much, nor see her so vividly, nor speculate about her so fruitlessly . . .

He placed the long-handled axe upright against the chopping-block, pulled the case without a lid towards him and tilted it up. It had probably been brought out here from the toolshed.

Covering the bottom was a heap of miscellaneous nuts and bolts, rusty and discarded, nails, screws, washers, angle-irons and brackets, pieces of wire and short lengths of narrow piping—all the typical oddments that are always put on one side instead of being thrown away, in the hope that one day they might prove useful.

On the top of the heap were broken chips and shavings of wood and—strangely and incongruously new—a small rectangular piece of what looked like celluloid or mica.

He lowered the end of the case and went back to his toolshed for a smaller cardboard box. He lifted the case and poured its contents into the box. One day when he had time he would sort it all out, keep what might be useful and throw the rest away.

Then he grasped the axe and set the case down on the floor. He put one foot firmly inside, and using the head as a hammer proceeded to smash the case into planks. These could be split later into kindling. Then he did the same with the other one. The lid he smashed as well. The smell of the disinfectant was not now so bad.

The wood was rotten and the heavy axe beautifully balanced. The task was not a hard one, but he worked in a frenzy to finish it quickly, using all his strength and littering the floor of the already untidy woodshed with even more splintered and broken pieces of wood.

It was as if he were finding an outlet for all his bewilderment, frustration and failure. He had talked to the men who had known her, but he had no more idea as to which one might have killed her than when he had started.

All that had happened—inexplicably and incredibly—was that she, who had been dead, seemed to come alive again—appealingly and enticingly, young, vital, fascinating and compelling—each time anyone mentioned her . . .

EIGHT

The same policeman in Locroix recognised him as he slowed down, and waved energetically, which not only made M. Pinaud feel considerably more cheerful but also convinced him that he was going to have a successful day.

He remembered the man's instructions from Wednesday and found a parking place without difficulty. Dufour had been as good as his word and the car had been ready as promised.

He locked the doors, took his case and invoice-book and walked back towards the intersection of the two main roads.

In the first shop, a harassed-looking individual in his shirt-sleeves was standing on a ladder half-way up one of the walls, which was almost completely covered with clocks. He was calling out their stock-numbers to a sexy-looking young girl who, seated on a high stool behind the counter, was engaged in ticking them off in a large ledger with a complete lack of interest.

She looked up at M. Pinaud with frank and open lust and made a big production of crossing her exquisite legs. He introduced himself politely and said his piece.

The man on the ladder shouted a number so suddenly that she jumped. To find the correct one and tick it in the book she was compelled to uncross her legs, since the stool was too high. This would give her the opportunity of recrossing them again later, and therefore she continued to eye him carnally, smiling wetly and lasciviously.

'All our clients and all our suppliers,' announced the man on the ladder, quietly at first and then with ever-mounting volume and exasperation, 'are fully aware that this is the one month in the year when we undertake our physical stock-taking. There is obviously no time to look at new samples. Even if there were, it would be pointless to do so, as no buying is ever done during stock-taking. If you care to come back next month, I cannot promise you and order, obviously, but at least I will look at your goods.'

Having said this, he climbed up carefully to the next step and shouted another number.

'Did you get that one, Francine?' he added.

'Yes, Papa,' she replied dutifully.

But Francine, it was not very difficult for M. Pinaud to recognize, was not really greatly interested either in her father or his stock of wall-clocks. Her lower body was already writhing in those enticing contortions which resulted in the crossing of her legs and it was perfectly obvious from her ardent and excited expression that, unlike her employer, what she wanted to look at most was certainly not M. Pinaud's samples...

He thanked them both politely, wondering if he were dreaming, and left the shop.

Outside, he made a note of the name and address. It

would be worth making another call next month. Her father might easily fall off the ladder and injure himself.

It should not be a task of insuperable difficulty, even to one with his limited experience of salesmanship, to sell Francine something . . .

In the next shop, which was considerably larger, he was informed by a very worried-looking manager that since three of his staff were away simultaneously with food-poisoning, there was no hope of doing any business for the moment.

M. Pinaud sympathized with him, said that naturally he quite understood the position and the manager's problems, and then proposed—perhaps because his mind was still filled with the enervating vision of those lovely silk-clad legs—that he call back next month, when he would almost certainly be again in Locroix.

The manager seemed pleased that he did not argue or insist, and they parted with expressions of mutual goodwill and esteem.

Outside M. Pinaud made another note.

The next jeweller he saw was neither harassed nor worried, but benignly complacent and terrifyingly eloquent.

The name of the firm was Claude and Rodin. He was Rodin. Unfortunately, Claude was on holiday. As they were partners, they made it a point of honour always to buy together, sharing their knowledge and a lifetime of experience to their mutual advantage.

All this in a deep, resonant and powerful voice, as if

he were reading a lesson in church, or even preaching the sermon.

There was not very much M. Pinaud could say. This was a statement of policy and fact. So he asked the obvious and only possible question.

'I see. And when will M'sieu Claude return from his holiday?'

'One week, maybe two—even three—who knows? You had better make it next month, M'sieu Pinaud. Come and see us then.'

'Thank you very much, M'sieu Rodin. I will do that.'

Another note outside. He should have bought a far larger notebook. Francine's father, even if he negotiated the climbing and the descending of his ladder with care and safety, might well drop down dead with a heart-attack after adding up the value of all the unsold clocks in his stock. If necessary, he might have to go to Locroix once a month to earn his living . . .

But in the fourth shop M. Théophile Honoré De La Haye was enthusiastic.

'These are the most beautiful rings I have ever seen in my life,' he declared. And in his voice M. Pinaud could distinguish appreciation, admiration and respect.

'Weight—design—workmanship—superb. Magnificent. I ought to know. I have my own goldsmith's diploma there on the wall.'

He gestured behind him, to where a magnificent long-case regulator stood in massive and yet graceful splendour behind the counter. He was a small man, mild and meek and inoffensive, but as he pointed to the dial and turned towards the clock, a great and inner pride seemed to add stature and an indefinable majesty to his presence.

'You see that? Read the name on the dial.'

M. Pinaud obediently moved nearer to do so, but M. De La Haye forestalled him by reading the inscription out aloud himself.

'The House of De La Haye. Clockmakers to the Kings of France. My great-grandfather made that clock, every wheel, pivot and pinion, all the screws and plates, on the bench we still keep here in the back of the shop.'

'What a marvellous clock,' said M. Pinaud reverently.

'But this is a craft that is dead. My grandfather—I would not say wasted—but spent his whole life trying vainly to keep it alive. My father had more sense. He started this shop. I realized when I left school that to run a shop needed specialized knowledge, so I studied and qualified as a goldsmith. But the competition in this town from the multiple shops makes things very difficult.'

M. Pinaud felt here that now was the time for him to start earning his living as a salesman.

'All the more reason, M'sieu De La Haye,' he pointed out swiftly, 'for you to have some of these magnificent rings in stock. The multiple shops here, with their headquarters in Paris, will never see them, let alone buy them. These rings are made by hand, individually. You will be able to show your clients something none of your competitors will ever have in stock.'

'I quite agree with you.'

M. De La Haye, now with his back to his great-grandfather's superb clock, seemed in some indefinable way to shrink back to become the man he had first been.

'But, unfortunately, there is nothing I can do about it.'

'What do you mean?'

'My wife, who is the principal shareholder in this business, has already agreed to sell the name and the goodwill to one of these multiple firms. She has no confidence in the future of this trade in these days of inflation. She wishes to have her money safe and secure for our old age. They will be taking over shortly. I very much regret that I no longer have any authority to buy, now that the balance-sheet and the existing stock-figures have been passed over by our accountant and accepted. It is a great pity that you did not come to see me some five years ago, M'sieu Pinaud.'

M. Pinaud agreed with him. It was indeed a pity, otherwise he might—no, he certainly would have obtained an order and earnt some commission.

But five years ago he was busily engaged in solving the complicated case of M. le Chef's murdered housemaid and dreaming of the days—which surely could not possibly be much longer delayed—when he would rightfully be hailed and acclaimed as the greatest detective of this modern age . . .

One could not be in two places at once. Who would have thought, at that time, that the most eminent of all the detectives in the *Sûreté* would now be trying to sell rings to earn a living?

It was a disturbing, and in some ways a sad thought. Life was indeed an incomprehensible thing.

There was really no point in pursuing his brief and yet interesting acquaintance with M. Théophile Honoré De La Haye. He therefore left him to th security and comfort of his wife's investments and went on to the next shop.

There a large and powerfully built character, exquisitely draped in an expensive suit, tilted back his small round head and eyed him contemptuously, as if sighting down the length of his long and narrow nose.

'I regret to inform you, M'sieu Pinaud, that here in this establishment we never buy goods in the summer. The summer is the season for selling. If you would care to call on us in the autumn, in September or October, we shall be delighted to look at your samples, in view of the approaching Christmas trade.'

So that was that. And that was also this, because this surely called for another note. In view of the manifold complications in his life these days, he knew very well that he would never be able to keep this character in mind until the autumn without a note. Swiftly he made one.

Mercifully, the next shop was only a few doors away, which meant that he was inside the entrance before he had found time to brood on this fresh disappointment.

M. Dupuis was short and aggressive, competent and assured. He listened politely to what M. Pinaud had to say, examined the rings swiftly and expertly and then studied the card between his fingers.

'This Armand Brissac—I have never heard of Vervion. He is a small man—business-wise?'

'Yes, m'sieu. It is his own firm and he runs it alone.'

'Then, on principle, I would never buy anything from him.'

'Why not?'

'One must have a repair-workshop in this trade.'

'He has his own. He is a practising and qualified goldsmith. He made these rings himself. There is no repair he could not handle.'

'Agreed. If I doubted that you were speaking the truth I have only to look once more at these rings. But this Brissac is running a one-man business in a small and isolated town—not only selling, but servicing and repairing as well. What if he gets really busy? What if I need one of these rings sized in a hurry? What if my client wants a diamond set in one of these signets in time for a birthday?'

'I can guarantee, M'sieu Dupuis, that M'sieu Brissac will give you as good a service as any wholesaler you are dealing with at present.'

'You are saying this, M'sieu Pinaud, for two reasons. The first is that you are loyal to M'sieu Brissac, your employer, which is a good and admirable thing. The second is that you want to sell me as many of these rings as possible, in order to earn your commission.

'I do not blame you. I am not condemning you. But I am a hard-headed businessman, and I look after my clients. Without difficulty I can foresee a situation in which M'sieu Brissac, solely because of his own personal circumstances and commitments, and through no ill-will on his part, could easily land both me and them in a proper mess.'

Here he shook his head decisively.

'No. The answer is no. In my opinion it is not worth risking. My principle still holds good. There must be the service of a fully equipped and competently organized workshop behind the sale of each ring, which is as important as the shank or the head—and as much a part of the article. My salary depends on the goodwill of my clients. My dealings with any one of them do not end with the sale of a ring. That transaction is only the beginning. It is what follows afterwards that is important. Far more important.'

He shook his head again with an even greater emphasis.

'I cannot fault your goods, M'sieu Pinaud. These are really beautiful rings. Nor your manner in presenting them. I am afraid—as I have tried to explain—that this is purely a matter of principle. Thank you for calling. I am sure you will have no difficulty in selling them elsewhere.'

Discouraged and down-hearted, he decided to call it a day. There were still more shops on which he had not called, but he felt that he had had enough.

There were so many things to do at home that he could not avoid the unpleasant thought that he was wasting his time here in Locroix. If he had been taking orders, that would have been different. But this—

The house-martins were no trouble. They nested underneath the gutters and built their nests high up and just below the projecting ledge of the pantile roof.

But the sparrows were maniacs. They were bringing straw and twigs above and sometimes even inside the gutters. After the long dry spell recently some of them had never seen the insides wet.

These last two days of heavy showers had caused chaos. Germaine had told him before he left that the main long gutter had overflowed at its end and that the water had been pouring down nearly all night into the base of their front room side door.

Setting off this morning, his mind preoccupied with optimistic estimates of the number of rings he was going to sell and fully exercised with all his conjectures as to how he was going to sell them, he had wilfully allowed the spate of her eloquence to flow like a spent and receding wave over the foreshore of his concentration.

He was Pinaud, the successful salesman. Well—perhaps in all honesty hardly very successful so far—but in his mind there was no doubt that shortly he would triumph. It was a new trade that he had to learn. When he first joined the *Sûreté* he did not know very much about detection. And look what had happened in twenty-five years.

Patience was essential. Patience and an unswerving dedication. Once he was successful—once and not if—with the prices of Brissac's rings he would be able to afford not one but several builders if necessary to clean out his gutters. It was all a matter of proportion.

At the moment it would be far more sensible if he went back home and cleaned them out himself.

Petrol was expensive. He looked at his fuel-gauge with dismay and headed for home.

His house was in the shape of a long rectangle, facing south, sheltered and protected by trees and shrubs, with the sheds built out at right angles in a line behind towards the north.

The church was quite near, on the other side of a narrow lane which led up from the by-road to the few houses grouped around it. On the far side of the church were the remaining houses and shops that comprised Vervion.

The approach to his front door was a path which crossed the lane and led to the church and the town.

After lunch, Germaine took her trowel and a bucket and departed to the far end of the garden to weed her flower-beds.

He changed his clothes and carried his ladder out to the narrow wall at the end of the house front. He extended it fully and set it up firmly on two wedges at the corner where the gutter had overflowed.

He rolled up the sleeves of his old shirt, fitted a butcher's hook into the handle of a bucket and climbed up—slowly and carefully and with some trepidation, since he was subject to vertigo—until his head was above the level of the gutter and he could see the cause of the trouble.

The gutter was choked with straw, twigs, leaves, bark, bird-droppings and pieces of decaying vegetation, all piled up to the very edge, so that the water from last night's rain was still dripping slowly but unendingly over the side. He could imagine the condition of the drain-pipe entry.

His hand was the best tool he could use. He scooped up the mess, a handful at the time, and quickly filled the bucket. Then he carried it down the ladder, very carefully, with its handle over his forearm to leave both hands free to hold on.

The compost-heap was at the far end of the garden. He carried the bucket there, emptied it and came back to continue. This was going to be a long and dirty job.

Flanking the side door of the front room, which was set in the narrow wall at the end, the previous owner had placed two enormous wine-barrels to act as water-butts. The drain-pipe from the gutter ran into one. Both lids were off, to catch as much as possible of the welcome rain that had been falling.

Rather than dirty his beautiful new ladder with this disgusting mess, he fetched a second bucket from the shed, drew off some water from one of the butts, and rinsed his hands before climbing up again to continue his task.

He did not work for very long.

He heard no sound of footsteps as a warning, but suddenly—violently and terrifyingly—the side of the ladder tilted fiercely and he completely lost his balance.

The sudden unexpectedness of it all caused him to lose simultaneously both his grip and his footing on the rung. With instinctive and almost instantaneous reaction his other hand caught at the gutter, but his feet were slipping as the rung tilted, and his weight tore the section of guttering, staples and all, out and away from the wall.

His other hand, with nothing to grasp, was free. With a savage contortion of his body, even as he felt himself falling, he twisted in mid-air, reached out and managed to grasp hold of the drain-pipe. But again, the staples in the wall had been designed for a specific purpose. To bear his weight was not one of them.

The ladder crashed one way to splinter on the concrete. M. Pinaud, in a shower of broken plaster, torn-out staples and odd sections of pipe and guttering, the other. Mercifully, his way led him feet first into the water-butt.

No blame can ever be attached to those medieval coopers, who had so proudly and lovingly soaked and bent and bound their staves with iron to contain so many hundred litres of good wine. M. Pinaud's weight, falling from almost the height of the gutter and accelerating so much per second, just made nonsense of any of their calculations as to stress per unit square.

He crashed into the water-butt and reduced it to matchwood with an indescribable noise. The staves split and splintered, the iron hoops bent, and most of the butt disintegrated. The water poured out all over the concrete floor of the courtyard.

When Germaine came, panting and running from the far end of the garden, her face as white as a sheet, he was able to stand proudly amidst the ruins of broken and shattered staves and ask for a pair of dry trousers.

'No,' he repeated to her for the third time, 'I did not hear a thing. Mind you, I was somewhat busy. I might tell you that this is not an easy task, scooping up handfuls of birds' muck in one's fingers with one's vision at eye-level over the edge of a gutter and the other hand gripping the ladder with some considerable nervous tension so as not to fall off.'

He had told her everything that had happened since the murder of Louise Voisin, as he had always told her, throughout their married life together, what had taken place and what was taking place during the development of any case, except naturally when he had been away from home.

'Someone in this place,' he continued, 'does not like me and my questions about Louise Voisin. Someone who would be quite happy if I accidently fell off a ladder, or hit another car when my steering failed, and spent a few months in hospital out of the way.'

'But—but surely I would have heard something. He may have crept down the path—but I came as soon as I heard the crash, and he must have run away—'

'Rubber shoes or crêpe soles—both are soundless,' he told her.

Macon had worn crêpe soles, he suddenly remembered. But if he were questioned, he would deny it. It was unlikely that anyone had seen him. In the middle of the afternoon in Vervion no-one had time to do anything else except get on with all the tasks a country life demanded. He would be wasting his time.

As Inspector Javel had said, there was no evidence.

NINE

Inside his beautifully appointed shop in Locroix, M. Latour listened the next day with courteous attention to what M. Pinaud had to say.

'Well then, M'sieu Pinaud—let us have a look at them. After that, perhaps I can tell you something. Until then, we are both wasting our time.'

M. Pinaud showed his rings.

M. Latour immediately became enthusiastic. He was a small man, beside M. Pinaud's bulk and stature, with a bland and cherubic countenance that did nothing to hide the penetrating shrewdness of his eyes.

'These are exceptionally beautiful rings,' he declared, after having held a glass to his eye to examine a few more closely. 'And the price of this one?'

M. Pinaud told him.

'Would you mind if I weighed one or two?'

'Not at all. Buying gold at the price it is to-day makes that your privilege. And you are buying them—I hope.'

The jeweller laughed as he took two rings to his scales at the back of the shop.

He adjusted the fine weights skilfully, with an

expertise born of a lifetime of experience. Then he came back to the counter, smiling cheerfully.

'Yes, M'sieu Pinaud. More than I thought. And I have had some experience. Your hope is a fact. Here you have something exceptional. I can always sell quality in this shop. My father and grandfather spent their lives in making it easy for me to do so. Now let us have a look at some of these shapes.'

Without hesitation he picked out ten of the heaviest and most expensive rings. M. Pinaud wondered if he were dreaming. Perhaps his fall into the water-butt—without breaking any bones—had given him concussion, and he no longer knew what was going on...

But he made a great effort to concentrate, and soon found himself writing in his invoice-book in his best handwriting and placing the rings chosen on a small tray over to the other side of the counter.

M. Latour was both charming and affable. He asked M. Pinaud several questions as to how he came to be travelling as an agent, and listened to the replies with an attentive and courteous interest.

'If I were you,' he told M. Pinaud when the latter had finished, 'I would think very seriously about carrying antiques. These are the things that will bring you real money. With inflation as it is to-day, more and more people are buying, as an investment, goods that will not depreciate in value as money is bound to do. Your only problem will be to find the right goods.'

'I know. But for that one needs expert knowledge. Otherwise one's prices can be completely wrong.'

As he spoke, M. Pinaud thought of the gutters, which he had not yet finished, of the woodshed, which he had not even started to re-organize, of the shrubs and bushes Germaine had told him were in the wrong places and therefore would have to be transplanted before the autumn, of the vegetable garden waiting to be dug and weeded, of the grass to be cut and the fence-posts painted—and of the hundred and one other tasks awaiting his hand.

He sighed heavily and continued quietly.

'I have no expert knowledge of antiques, M'sieu Latour. I would have to educate myself before I could even begin to make a living. That would take time. At the present moment that is the one thing I do not have.

'My wife and I have recently moved into a lovely old house in Vervion, but after some six hundred years, in spite of our builder's most successful efforts, there are still now and obviously always will be things that need attention. My time, I can see, will be fully occupied. But may I say how much I appreciate your good advice and your kindness and generosity in giving it to me.'

'It was a pleasure. I would like to see you earning more. I am afraid this is not a very large order, but these rings are expensive and there is a limit as to how many I can carry in stock.

'By the way, would you ask your M'sieu Brissac if he would be prepared to make some new designs—completely different from these orthodox shapes—something that the young people to-day designate as wayout or *outré*. I have an idea—more than an idea, it is a conviction—that I could sell them here. After all, it is the young people who have the money to-day. Listen to what he says about the idea. If, as you tell me, he makes these exquisite rings because he enjoys making them, you will have no difficulty in persuading him.

'Come and see me next time with them, M'sieu Pinaud, and I can almost certainly guarantee you another order.'

He walked out of the shop as if treading on air. This was the life.

Why on earth had he not spent his own in selling things—it was so easy with the right people—rather than in driving about like a lunatic—wearing out his beautiful car—tracking down and chasing murderers and perverts and torturers and sadists, and always getting mixed up, as Inspector Javel had been at pains to point out, with naked or half-naked girls who had only one object in mind?

As one gets older, he reflected ruefully, so life seems to get more incomprehensible.

The next shop, Rougement, was small and empty. It remained empty for some considerable time, even though the bell had rung as he opened the door.

Then, very slowly and very quietly, a lady came through the arched entrance from the back. She had iron-grey hair and what would normally have been sweet and happy features, but which were now lined and ravaged with a terrible grief. Her eyes were red and swollen. She had obviously been crying.

M. Pinaud opened his mouth to say his piece and then changed his mind. When he spoke his words were entirely different.

'Madame,' he said, quietly and with a great sincerity, 'You are obviously upset. I will not trouble you this morning. Perhaps I could call again later—'

She had been looking at him without understanding. Perhaps it was the genuine sympathy in his voice that enabled her to see him for the first time.

'My husband died three days ago,' she whispered to interrupt him sadly.

'I am very sorry to hear that, Madame,' he told her, and again the sympathy and the sincerity in his voice seemed to reach out gentle, soothing and comforting hands to enfold and assuage her pain and sorrow. 'Then you will not wish to be troubled by me. May I ask—did he suffer?'

'No. It was quick and merciful. He had a heart-attack.'

'For that—although it is not easy—one should be thankful. That is the right way to go. There is no greater agony than having to watch a loved one suffering while dying slowly and inevitably. In your great sorrow, Madame, there can be little of comfort, but try to remember, if you can, that this you were spared. You may even find some measure of peace in the thought.'

Now she looked at him attentively, wondering and with a new interest.

'You are a very unusual man,' she said quietly, having finished her careful appraisal. 'So refreshingly different from the usual type of commercial traveller who used to see my husband.'

'Indeed?' he asked politely. If the politeness was vague and conversational, he should not be blamed. It was a remark almost impossible to answer.

'Yes. They came to see my husband, naturally, since he did the buying, but I often had occasion to pass them and hear what they were saying as I went through here to serve a client in the shop.'

For the first time the shadow of a very faint smile touched her lips.

'You would not believe what remarkable types are representing respectable and established firms to-day. Mind you, I admit that I am very possibly old-fashioned—which certainly makes it so much harder for me when I look in vain for some of that bygone courtesy which used to be the life-blood of business relations.

'To-day, they all seem to wear the same smart suits and loud ties. They all carry sample-cases in black leather with chrome-plated locks. They all need a haircut. Many have beards, to save valuable time by not shaving. They all have fast cars, for which they have not saved up and paid, and continually boast about the fantastic speeds and mileages they record. And none of them seem to have any manners. Brash, I believe, is the modern word.'

Again that same shadow of a smile touched her lips. He was pleased to see it. Three days added up to a long time without a smile.

'But then, as I said, I am almost certainly old-fashioned. I look for things which no longer exist. I tend to forget that we have been here for a very long time. We moved into these premises some thirty-seven years ago, three days after our honeymoon started. It was my father-in-law's business, and it was his wish, and also a condition of his will, that we should never close the shop in the event of his illness or death.

'Naturally we honoured his wish. It has been a lifetime of hard work, but we did make a success of it.'

'I am sure you did, Madame.'

He gestured with his hand around him—to the well-appointed and gleaming show-cabinets, to the small and tasteful display counters, to the few superb long-case clocks and the one magnificent mahogany shelf holding alarm and repeating carriage-clocks—in one sweeping and comprehensive gesture.

'And I congratulate you. And there is one other thing of which I am sure.'

She was looking at him now, he was pleased to see, not with grief and sorrow, but with a definite interest.

'And that is—'

'I know for a fact that over the long years of such an achievement together you and your husband must surely both have regained far more of whatever happiness you may have lost by curtailing your honeymoon.'

For a long moment there was silence. Then she smiled, sweetly and proudly.

'Thank you,' she said simply. 'What a charming thought. You are quite right.'

And then she added:

'And to think I do not even know your name, m'sieu.'

'It is Pinaud, Madame.'

She stared.

'Are you any relation to that celebrated detective in the *Sûreté*?'

He laughed.

It was a loud laugh and a brave laugh—loud enough to conceal the sudden emotion that misted his eyes, and brave in its acceptance of the irony of a fate that could demand a lifetime of ceaseless endeavour and devoted striving, a long and continual battle with horror and danger, death and disaster, and in return could only offer—instead of fame, riches and recognition—one of these typically casual and extremely rare moments of ecstatic happiness at sincere appreciation from a member of his microscopic public . . .

'More than a relation, Madame. I am that Pinaud—or rather, I was until quite recently. There has been a reorganization and I was asked to retire.'

'But how extraordinary. I have read many of your adventures. They are all in the public library here in Locroix. My husband and I'—here her eyes filled with tears, but quickly and hardly she wiped them with a handkerchief—'both enjoyed them immensely.'

'Thank you.'

'Did you write them yourself?'

'No, Madame. I have a faithful chronicler. To him it is a labour of love.'

'How fascinating—that I should actually meet you in person.'

Her features now were animated and vivacious. And in consequence, compellingly attractive. She was like a different woman. Then she looked at the small case he was still holding under his arm.

'Then now—what are you doing—if you are no longer with the *Sûreté*?'

Until this morning, honesty would have compelled him to word his answer differently. Now, thanks to M. Latour, he could reply not only with complete veracity, but even with a great and justifiable pride.

'I am selling the most magnificent hand-made rings,

Madame, acting as an agent on commission. They are made individually by our local goldsmith in Vervion, and they are so beautiful that they have to be seen to be believed.'

She smiled—now fully and completely. This was a man after her own heart.

'Well then—I must certainly see them, M'sieu Pinaud. But may I ask you to be patient for another few weeks—until I have seen the lawyers and my accountants and all the decisions have been made as to whether I shall continue to manage the business here. Do you mind?'

'Of course not. I quite understand. There will be a great deal of work for you, Madame, and I sincerely hope that everything will be settled satisfactorily. I will telephone at the end of the month to hear when it will be convenient for me to see you.'

He bowed with a natural dignity and perfect grace.

'It has been a great pleasure for me to meet you, Madame. Good-bye for now. My good wishes remain with you.'

As he closed the front door behind him, he thought that perhaps he should have some new business-cards printed with his name in the centre. In the lower left-hand corner there would be: Agent for Armand Brissac, Goldsmith of Vervion. And in the opposite right-hand corner could be: Late of the *Sûreté*.

From what had just happened, it seemed that this modest advertisement might pay handsome dividends. Obviously, some people—however few—must have read of his exploits over the long years, as this charming lady had done, or else his chronicler would never have found the courage to go on writing about so many—to say nothing of typing each manuscript laboriously with his two forefingers . . .

On the way back to Vervion, through the rolling farmland countryside, the clutch on his car started to slip.

He swung out to pass a lorry and the engine raced but the car did not accelerate. He changed down swiftly and managed to obtain enough extra speed to pass.

Afterwards, once the driver of the lorry had given up chasing him in frustrated rage, with the huge radiator almost touching his rear number-plate, and turned off into a farm entrance, he slowed and drove gently and cautiously, trying to avoid putting any undue stress on the clutch, which was obviously failing.

This is a fine thing, he thought bitterly and savagely. What on earth is the use of earning commission—if it is all going into Dufour's pocket? I have not even had his first bill for the back axle. Nor his second one for the tow and the steering. If only that idiot M. le Chef had listened to me and given me a new car when I asked for it.

He drove on, slowly and carefully, his ears attentive and alert for the first warning of what was bound to be a major breakdown, his mind a turmoil of bitter and frustrating thoughts.

The car still cruised, at a moderate speed, quietly and efficiently. On acceleration it failed, as if his engine were labouring to drive another car.

The kilometres passed, one after the other. Germaine and home came ever nearer. Gradually, with a great and agonizing difficulty, he forced himself to relax. If only he could get the car to Dufour, he would be all right. The man might be a murderer, but he was also a good mechanic. He would know what to do. He would repair the clutch-plates, or fit a new clutch, without any trouble, and then he could go back to Locroix and sell more rings and earn more commission—if only to pay more bills.

He came to the last long hill. Vervion lay huddled in the sheltered valley on the far side of its crest. He wondered which gear it would take to get him over the top.

As he began the climb he heard the unmistakable and characteristic *whoosh* of a rocket fired from the copse on his right. The road was clear, so he stole a glance to see who could have fired it, but the small cluster of trees seemed deserted. There was no sign of any human being.

At the height of its trajectory, a cluster of coloured stars burst out violently, vivid against the soft clear blue of the summer sky.

Then, guiltily, he lowered his eyes and concentrated on his driving. This hill was both long and steep, and doubled back and forth in a series of hair-pin bends to reduce the gradient. He changed down again, nursing his engine, and wondered if he would ever get to the top.

It was strange to see a rocket on a week-day in the middle of early summer—and in the heart of the country. He could not recall that there were any Saints Days, feast-days or public holidays this week. And in his youth children had always capered about the base of the rocket-stick until long after the final stars had fallen, and even stood in motorists' path, with their caps held out in front of them, if only with the laudable ambition of trying to defray some of their expenses in buying the rocket.

The road curved again as he came to the summit of the hill—curved in a long blind corner that seemed to lead endlessly to the crest. He reduced his speed—only slightly, because he was still on the gradient, and followed the high hedge that marked the right-hand contour of the road.

From behind its dense foliage he heard the chattering clatter of a tractor's diesel engine approaching him.

The curve continued, and then suddenly the hedge ended. And there, coming out of the field footpath, steeply downhill and straight at him, was the tractor.

By itself it would have been a sufficiently intimidating sight, since it was a large one and on the wrong side of the road, roaring directly at him. What made it even more terrifying was the immense and fearsome iron roller, with gigantic steel tines attached, protruding from its side.

There was literally no road left. The whole incredible contraption clattered and roared swiftly towards him.

He did the only thing possible to avoid the menace of those fearful tines.

With incredible speed, in the split seconds remaining, he thrust the car into low gear, tore the wheel hard over to the left, and with screaming and smoking tyres shot head-first across the road into what he hoped would be the safety of another field. Perhaps there would be a ditch, as there had been the time before. In any case, it was worth trying. And it was the only thing to do.

But on the way he crossed two massive and completely concealed boulders. Together they snapped his track-rod, garnished with Dufour's new split-pin, like a piece of rotten firewood, so that turning the wheel had no longer the slightest effect on his steering.

With the power of that frantic surge of acceleration, even with the brake hard down, he roared straight on, completely out of control, right into the trunk of a massive elm-tree.

The windscreen starred into opaqueness, but did not splinter. The safety-belt stretched sufficiently under the terrific strain to enable him to bang his head sharply on his driving-mirror. His diaphragm met the lower rim of the steering-wheel with enough violence to temporarily wind him and his knees hit the edge of the dashboard with considerable force.

The elm-tree stood as it had done for five hundred years, towering, majestic and invincible. With time the wounds would heal, new wood and new bark would grow.

First of all, through the partially open window, he became aware of the utter silence. His own engine had stopped and the puttering roar of the diesel had ceased. Not only the tranquil countryside but the whole world—apart from him—was sleeping.

Then, in a swift moment of blind and almost uncontrollable panic, intensified out of all proportion by his vivid imagination, he wondered whether the doors had jammed with the impact against the tree, and how long it would be before the petrol from some fractured pipe reached the hot exhaust and the whole thing burst into flames before he could get out . . .

He tried the driver's door. The handle was fixed and immovable. Twisting and leaning forward with what he hoped was urgency and not panic, he tried the opposite front door, and then, kneeling on the seat, both back ones. They were all jammed, tightly closed, solid.

He was glad and thankful to see the farmer outside the window, grasping an enormous tyre-lever in his brown and massive hands.

'Are you hurt, m'sieu?'

'No,' he gasped. 'I don't think so.'

'Then you had better get out—quick. I have seen before what happens next.'

The farmer tried the outside door handle once. Then he braced himself firmly against the rear door, jammed in the end of the tyre-lever and with an incredibly powerful heave tore the whole lock and catch bodily out of their housing.

'Quick—out,' he repeated. 'Any moment now. Do you want any help?'

'No, thank you.'

He remembered to take his sample case of rings and his invoice-book from the seat beside him. In spite of his denial, he was thankful for the farmer's arm, which supported him like a bar of iron.

A tongue of flame licked up and out of the ventilation grill.

They walked clear quickly and from a safe distance watched the blazing wreck that had once been M. Pinaud's beloved car.

'You will get the insurance, m'sieu,' declared the farmer cheerfully. 'Not even the most bloody-minded of all insurance companies can possibly argue with this one. It was my fault entirely. The accelerator jammed and the brakes failed on my tractor—hydraulic pipes are tricky things. I was too worried to look at the road and see what was coming. I am your witness, when you fill in the claim. My name is Nardin. I farm down this side of the hill as far as Vervion.'

'Mine is Pinaud. We moved into the old house opposite the church a few months ago.'

'I know that. In Vervion we all know everything.'

He was a tall and powerfully built individual of middle-age, with a skin like leather and, when he smiled, startingly white and ill-fitting false teeth.

He displayed them now.

'You will have no more worries about repair-bills,' he continued with undiminished optimism. 'My friend Dufour has told me all about them. Your car there is a complete write-off. It was quite an old one, and so they will obviously try very hard to fob you off with market-value, which is nothing.'

He glanced shrewdly at the sample-case M. Pinaud held under his arm.

'Traveller?'

'Yes.'

'Then you must insist on a replacement car—essential for you to earn your living. Get a good lawyer if necessary and let him earn his fee. I will sign whatever he wants.'

He smiled again cheerfully and waved the tyre-lever to where his tractor lurched drunkenly amidst the wreckage of what had once been a magnificent hedge.

'My own insurance company is not going to be too pleased with me, I can tell you. Not only the tractor, but your car and the hedge as well. My grandfather planted that one. It is worth a fortune as a wind-break. But who cares for them? They are always happy enough to take your money as a premium once a year.'

He paused and looked carefully at M. Pinaud.

'Would you like to come back to the farm with me, M'sieu Pinuad, and have a drink? You are looking rather white and shaken—which is not surprising. It is not far.'

M. Pinaud looked at him thoughtfully.

He had never before heard of a tractor's accelerator and brakes failing simultaneously, although he would have been the first to admit that he knew very little about the system or the functioning of hydraulic power.

And in all his long life he had never before seen a rocket fired in daylight in the middle of a deserted countryside without some good and valid reason for celebration. If it had been a signal, then the estimated time of his arrival at the top of the hill could have been calculated very closely.

And if this farmer was the one from whom the proprietor of The Seven Sons of Aymon purchased that incredible liqueur, which was quite likely, then obviously what he retained for his own consumption and delight and did not sell, would certainly be far stronger and tastier, and therefore far more capable of masking the taste of whatever might be unobtrusively dropped into his glass before he drank . . .

And then he remembered how this man had appeared almost at once, with a tyre-lever in his hand, and suddenly all his suspicions seemed mean and contemptible, like the petty spite of a vindictive child.

He shook his head slowly.

'Thank you for the kindness of your offer, M'sieu Nardin—but I can assure you that I am feeling all right. And I would like to get home as soon as possible —before my wife has a chance to worry.'

'Of course. If we stand in the road here, anyone coming up the hill is bound to be going into Vervion. No-one has passed yet—there is sure to be a car soon. There—there you are. Here is the postman from Locroix on the lower bend. He will give you a lift.'

'M'sieu Nardin—' he began. Then he paused, seeking for the right words.

'Yes?'

'Before he gets here—there is something that must be said, even though words are often sadly inadequate things. But—but may I shake your hand—and thank you for saving my life—'

'Of course.'

Not even the white and ill-fitting teeth could mask the sincerity of his smile.

'Think nothing of it. It was all my fault. I got you into the mess. The least I could do was to get you out of it. You were lucky—you could have been badly hurt—or even dead.'

'Yes.'

M. Pinaud's voice was expressionless as he replied. 'It is of that I am thinking.'

They shook hands warmly, two strong men brought together by fate and circumstance, drawn and attracted by a mutual esteem and admiration.

'Walk up one day when you have nothing else to do,' the farmer told him with another smile. 'The drink is not only against the walls of the cellar, but all over the floor as well. There is surely enough for two.'

'Thank you. I will do that.'

And then the postman stopped his van in answer to their hail, and took him down to Vervion.

TEN

'Ah yes, M'sieu Pinaud,' said Inspector Javel, with as much lack of expression in his voice as was apparent in his pale grey eyes. 'You notified us last night of your accident and the total loss of your car by fire. But you gave no details, no particulars. And you requested this appointment and interview this afternoon. Now what is it you wished to see me about?'

He was exactly as M. Pinaud remembered him—calm, unmoved and disinterested.

He leaned forward from behind his desk in that plain and bleak office on the first floor, and managed to convey successfully—without recourse either to speech or expression—that M. Pinaud's affairs, whatever he thought of them, were of comparatively insignificant import beside those of a thriving municipality such as Vervion.

'The correct answer to that,' M. Pinaud replied blandly, 'Is obviously the still unsolved murder of one Louise Voisin in my woodshed.'

He knew now suddenly that he was at his best. After these last few days of anxiety, frustration and bewilderment, he now felt, in surprising contrast, a surge of power and confidence coursing through every vein in his body.

He sat back in his chair, massive and confident, completely self-assured and—although he did not know it—awe-inspiringly formidable.

'Mind you, Inspector Javel,' he continued, 'I am the first to admit that I am probably the only man in Vervion to see any connection with her and what I am about to tell you—'

'And what is that?' the inspector interrupted quickly.

'Some very strange things have been happening here in this town since I began asking a few questions about her death,' M. Pinaud told him quietly. 'I took my car in to Dufour for repairs to the back axle. On my way back from Montville the other day the steering failed and I ended up in a ditch. Apparently the split-pin which secures the steering assembly had either worn out or been filed and removed. I was lucky to escape with my life.'

'Indeed?'

The inspector's question was courteous but without any special interest. These things, one would gather from his tone, do happen. M. Pinaud did not agree. If they happened, there had to be a reason.

'There is not much point in saying indeed, Inspector Javel,' he said deliberately, and quite unconsciously there was a hardness in his voice that brought the inspector forward to sit rigidly on the edge of his chair. 'You yourself were the one who told me that Dufour was a suspect.'

'Agreed. One of several. If I told you that he was a

suspect, then you can take my word that he is. But if you will remember, M'sieu Pinaud, I also told you that there was no evidence against any of these suspects. Did you get some? Have you any concrete proof for me, on which I can take action? Did you examine the split-pin before you left his garage?'

'Of course not. The repairs were to the back axle. Why should I? When you go to the dentist—do you ask him to syringe out your ears? He maintains that the pin may have corroded with age.'

'Then you see what I mean.'

M. Pinaud looked at him directly in the eyes, trying vainly to read any expression in their pale and colourless depths.

'I do not,' he replied shortly. 'But let us continue. The day before yesterday I came back from Locroix. In the afternoon I climbed up a ladder to clean out my gutter. My wife was at the far end of the garden. Someone came up the path from the church, very quietly and without a sound—probably on crêpe soles —opened the two gates without making any noise, which was not difficult since I keep the latches and hinges well oiled, and jerked the ladder away while I was at the top. I did not hear a sound, neither of anyone coming nor going. I was lucky enough to fall into the water-butt—otherwise this interview would have taken place in hospital.'

There was a long silence. Inspector Javel did not say indeed—which was just as well, M. Pinaud reflected, or else he might have been strangled.

Instead he evinced, if not interest, at least attention.

'Crêpe soles—of course. That would be logical.'

'Robert Macon was wearing crêpe-soled boots when I saw him.'

'That means nothing. Anyone can buy a pair and keep them handy if the need arises. General Correvon wears leather shoes with iron studs and heel-bars—he still dreams he is reviewing his troops on the parade-ground—but he does not have to wear them every day.'

'It must have been someone completely familiar with the path and my house and garden.'

'Naturally. All the suspects qualify.'

'Someone who could walk down that path confidently, as if on some visit to a neighbour, wait if necessary, concealed behind the laurel bushes until I was up, see that there was no-one approaching, and then run in. And afterwards walk on towards the copse and the stream to rejoin the road.'

'Exactly. You have reconstructed the situation admirably.'

The inspector leaned back placidly in his chair.

'But unfortunately that does not help us at all.'

'What do you mean? Someone here in this place tried to kill me—or at least put me out of action.'

'Agreed. But as I said before—where is your proof? Where is your evidence for me to make a charge? Did your wife see him? Did you see him? I am quite prepared to knock on the doors of all the houses around you and even the priest's house by the church—but what shall I say? Excuse me, m'sieu or madame, but did you see anyone loitering outside, with felonious intent, on the path near M'sieu Pinaud's house on the afternoon of the eighteenth—at what time shall I say, M'sieu Pinaud? Some time in the afternoon. We do not even know the time. I am not blaming you. One does not usually time the operation of cleaning out a gutter.'

He leaned forward again in his chair, vital and compelling and convincing.

'But the point I am trying to make, M'sieu Pinaud, is that five or six people may have been seen walking down that path by the church after lunch. All had some legitimate reason—all except one. None will deny their presence there in answer to my questions, particularly if they were seen—and especially not the one who came soundlessly and specifically into your garden to knock you off your ladder. He will have the most convincing reason of all of them.'

It was perhaps understandable that M. Pinaud should experience some of the frustration and exasperation of trying to grasp a wet fish or a slippery eel in his hand. What aggravated his annoyance so intensely was that the inspector was completely correct, logical and convincing in what he said. But that did not help anyone, least of all him.

He made a great effort to master and control his emotions.

'I see what you mean,' he said slowly. 'Then let me tell you now what happened yesterday. I was coming back from Locroix. As I approached the hill towards the crest, someone let off a rocket—an ordinary cheap rocket with two or three coloured stars before the final burst of golden rain. Clearly visible as a signal against the clear summer sky. But obviously not half as effective or spectacular as letting it off at night, which is the normal time to celebrate victories, Saints Days, and other special occasions with fireworks.'

He paused for a moment to emphasize his next words.

'Of which there were none yesterday. I took the time and the trouble to verify that fact on the calendar before I came here. I looked from the car but did not see anyone. Which was not surprising. There is plenty of cover on either side of that road.

'At the top of the hill a tractor with some devilish great iron roller sticking out of its side suddenly came out of a field right in my path. I had to be quick to avoid a head-on collision, and so I turned my car off the road. I think I must have hit some hidden stones which smashed my steering, so I could not help bashing into a tree. The car caught fire and is a wreck.

'The farmer who got me out—the doors were jammed—gave his name as Nardin. Does that ring a bell? Is he also on the list of your suspects? He claims that both his accelerator jammed and his brakes failed at the same time—which I would say at a conservative estimate are odds of several thousands to one against, admits cheerfully that it was entirely his own fault and maintains that he will advise his own insurance company to that effect.'

Inspector Javel, who had been sitting listening with his own special brand of bored indulgence which M. Pinaud found so infuriating, reacted at once to the mention of the name Nardin.

He sat up straight in his chair and visibly tensed, but did not say anything until M. Pinaud had finished speaking.

'Now that—' he began slowly, and then suddenly continued to speak very rapidly.

'That, M'sieu Pinaud, is extremely interesting.'

'Why should you say that?'

'Because Jules Nardin has a young son. Some two years ago the boy caught pneumonia, and it was only due to Doctor Poidevin's devoted care and attention during the crisis that the boy is alive to-day. He has completely recovered, and is a normal and healthy child—just the type to spend his pocket-money on buying a rocket.'

For a moment there was silence. M. Pinaud did not speak. Then Inspector Javel continued:

'What I am trying to tell you, M'sieu Pinaud, is this —that to a man of Nardin's type, an obligation is both an honour and a necessity. If—let us just at this point only say if, because there is no proof and no evidence— if he were asked to do a favour for the doctor who came and sat day and night by the child's bedside—do you think he would refuse? Of course not. He would welcome the chance to repay some of his debt.'

M. Pinaud thought very carefully.

'Yes,' he agreed at last, slowly and with emphasis. 'That fits in with his character, as far as I could estimate it. His object was probably to wreck my car and put me out of action for a while, but definitely not to kill me. Why should he kill me? He did not even know me. Repaying an obligation to his friend Poidevin should not call for murder. When he saw that I would almost certainly have been roasted alive, he risked his own life to come to help me.'

'Agreed,' said the inspector quietly. 'He is that type. A good one.'

Then for a long moment there was silence between

them. M. Pinaud was busy with his own thoughts. Inspector Javel did not say anything.

Then, suddenly, the inspector stirred in his chair and spoke. M. Pinaud had the impression that the silence, for him, had inexplicably become unendurable.

'Have you ever considered the fact, M'sieu Pinaud,' he asked quietly and reasonably, 'that you might be one of those persons who are accident-prone? From what you have just told me I would not think it to be an unreasonable assumption. Some people, particularly those who have lived violent and dangerous lives, seem unable to avoid them.'

M. Pinaud frowned.

'I do not think so for a moment,' he replied shortly. 'All my violent and dangerous life has done over the years is to make me more careful. Otherwise I can assure you that I would not be sitting in this chair now. Since I am doing so, I think you will agree that I am entitled to know what you intend doing about these— these attempts to put me out of action, any one of which, I do not have to tell you, might easily have resulted in murder.'

Inspector Javel's expression did not change.

'Nothing,' he replied.

'But—'

'I said nothing,' he interrupted, 'For the good, plain and simple reason that there is nothing to be done. I thought I had made that completely clear, M'sieu Pinaud.

'Whatever ideas and convictions you may have brought to this small place with you from the *Sûreté*, I would like to point out that here none of them apply. There is no question of police procedure. There are, as yet, not even enough grounds for official questioning. Being under suspicion is not a criminal offence—not until the suspicion has been formally alleged and proved correct. This I am unable to do.'

He leaned back in his chair and placed his fingertips together.

'Dufour will maintain that he was repairing your back axle and did not even think of checking your steering. You did not ask him to. Then why should he? As the finest mechanic in the whole *Département*, he does not have to solicit or create work. It comes to him.

'I have already told you about all the people who could have come down your path and knocked you off your ladder. I can waste my time, if you wish, in questioning them. The answers will all be ready from the guilty one, planned beforehand. There is no evidence, no proof. With your taxes you pay my salary. I am a servant of the public. If you wish me to waste my time and your money I am quite prepared to do so.

'Jules Nardin will swear that he could not see your car coming up the hill because of the hedges and trees. The noise of his own engine would have prevented him from hearing you. And you can be sure that if there were any throttle linkages to be jammed or hydraulic pipes to be fractured, they would have been competently attended to well before he got his tractor towed to Dufour's garage.

'His son will have school-friends willing to swear that he spent the whole afternoon walking with them, since it is holiday time, and that none of them get enough pocket-money to afford rockets, which cost considerably more than sweets.

'And anyone—I say anyone advisedly—might have telephoned Madame your wife from a public call-box, given another name and ascertained that you had gone to Locroix, but were expected back for lunch. After that, it would have been only a question of watching the one road back and awaiting your arrival up the hill.'

Again there was a long silence between them. M. Pinaud made a great and praiseworthy attempt to marshall all his chaotic thoughts into an orderly sequence.

'Then,' he asked quietly, 'for the second time may I ask what are you going to do, Inspector Javel? How are you going to spend the taxpayers' money? What progress have you made, and what ideas do you entertain, about solving this brutal murder of a young girl?'

The inspector met his searching gaze frankly, but to M. Pinaud it was as if he were staring into an opaque sheet of glass. There was no expression at all in the pale grey eyes. The voice replied to him and answered his question, but it might as well have come from a different person.

'I am doing my best, M'sieu Pinaud. I am proceeding in accordance with all the established and well-documented rules of detection. I propose to be perfectly frank with you and inform you that so far my investigations have yielded nothing. There is no proof, no evidence—as I told you before. And what is more, I have no hesitation in admitting that I doubt if there ever will be.

'As you rightly pointed out yourself, it is perfectly obvious that the guilty person has been upset and alarmed by your interest and your questions and intends to see that you do not continue with them. If you should get discouraged by these accidents and decide to move back to Paris, it will not be easy for you to continue with your enquiries. From a hospital bed you might find it even more difficult.'

'Everything you have told me,' M. Pinaud replied, 'is eminently reasonable. Perhaps you will forgive me, nevertheless, if I insist on making two points. The first is that with all the numerous suspects you had no hesitation in pointing out to me, surely it can only be a simple matter of logical elimination to find out the guilty one.

'The second is that if you would take the trouble to contact my chronicler, who is a most obliging person, and read a few of my many adventures, you will realize that not once but many times I have solved cases of murder with far less evidence—to say nothing of a complete absence of suspects—than you have at present before you.

'These comments are made—I hasten to assure you, Inspector Javel—in no spirit of condemnation or denigration, but only to encourage you to continue with your investigations.'

His tone was both civil and polite. If an edge of steel lay beneath the words, this might be discovered later by repeating them again, but without re-examination it was not immediately discernible.

Inspector Javel decided to take them at face value.

'What you have said is quite true. But try to realize that I am not making excuses, but trying to offer explanations. Suspicions are not enough. I must have evidence or proof. So far I have found none. That does not mean that I have given up, nor that I have ceased trying. I have my own ideas about this crime, and I am pursuing them in my own way.

'There are certain things about which I would like to know a good deal more, and this I intend to find out. One is about the considerable sum of money which Armand Brissac needed in a hurry quite recently—'

'He told me about that,' M. Pinaud interrupted with interest.

'Maybe he did. After all, why not? You are working for him, I hear. I am only investigating a murder. He did not tell me. I found out by other methods. I hope to find out more.

'And another thing I would like to know is why Dufour's wife, who is devoted to her mother and often goes to see her, should have chosen that particular Sunday, two weeks ago, to visit her at Pontlieu and leave him alone.'

'You mean the Sunday—'

'Yes. The Sunday on which Louise Voisin was almost certainly murdered.'

'He told me she went again last Sunday.'

The inspector's voice was as expressionless as his eyes.

'Did he? Then it is even more strange, that she should have gone twice. Perhaps he has mixed up his Sundays. And also I would like to know why young

Robert Macon is continually talking about expanding his father's business, and yet so far has made no definite propositions to get a loan to do so. And in addition why General Correvon has not yet accepted the very lucrative appointment which his wife, because of her influence with a certain minister, has finally succeeded in obtaining for him.'

He paused and sighed.

'These, M'sieu Pinaud, are all things which I have to do and certainly shall do in the execution of my duty. In addition, I shall make a point of having an informal talk with the young Nardin boy about rockets, most certainly not in the presence of his parents. Young people, I have found, are not at their best under intensive questioning. Their anxiety is obvious and they lack the experience to lie skilfully and convincingly.'

He paused again, hesitated, and then stood up behind his desk.

'I can assure you, M'sieu Pinaud,' he added, 'that in spite of your observations and comments, I am not wasting my time.'

M. Pinaud stood up as well. He gathered he was being told politely that the interview was over and therefore there was nothing else to do.

It was a pity, he thought, that between them there should be this lack of understanding, sympathy and co-operation. He had given the best years of his life to the enforcement of law, order and justice. This man, far younger—keen, competent and ambitious—was doing the same thing. And yet from the beginning they had seemed unable to approach each other.

Perhaps, he thought swiftly, it was his own fault. He

had never taken kindly to being considered a suspect himself. Perhaps it was that—a natural resentment—which had put him so much on the defensive right from the beginning of their acquaintance.

And yet, in all fairness, he was bound to admit that the inspector's inferences had been both reasonable and logical. In his place he himself would probably have thought the same.

'Good,' he replied, without any expression at all. Then his voice suddenly changed as he continued, giving each word a sincerity and a conviction that were overwhelmingly impressive.

'And let me too assure you of something, Inspector Javel. I would like you to know that in spite of all these attempts, either to kill me or put me out of action, I am still determined—more than ever now—to go on with my own questions and my own investigations, until I have finally found out the truth. I shall not give up until I know who is the murderer of Louise Voisin. Good-day to you, Inspector.'

ELEVEN

This time he addressed the proprietor of The Seven Sons of Aymon with the cordiality of an old friend.

The last time he had been inside the *café* this individual had trusted him with a full bottle of that delectable apple liqueur and had replenished his pot with fresh hot coffee without being asked.

That was the occasion on which he had decided to become a salesman. In these depressing days of inflation, profiteering and self-seeking, it was a refreshing change to meet a host who had obviously been brought up in the correct and traditional manner of considering the welfare and the comfort of his guests as the most important of all his obligations.

Now he spoke with his best smile.

'Good-evening to you, m'sieu. I do not know if you remember me—'

'Of course I do. It is M'sieu Pinaud.'

'Right. I ordered then a pot of very strong black coffee. At that time I had a problem. And you gave me a bottle of liqueur which I shall never forget. With the help of both my problem was solved.'

'I am glad to hear you say that, m'sieu. Not many

clients would be generous enough to take the trouble and devote their time to come here specially to tell me such a thing. Then Inspector Javel has found out who murdered the girl in your woodshed?'

'No. He has not. And in my opinion—between you and me—he never will. But that is not what I meant. Now I have other problems. Now I have a purple weal across my diaphragm, a bruise on my forehead as you can see, and no skin on my knees, as if the splitting of a perfectly good pair of trousers were not enough. I was in a car accident yesterday, and lucky to escape with my life.'

'I congratulate you, m'sieu.'

'Thank you. Now I have to think. I do not expect you to improve on the quality of your coffee or your liqueur —that would be impossible—but if you would be kind enough to bring me the same again, I have no doubt at all that they will help me to solve these new problems of mine in exactly the same way as they did before. That is why I am here.'

'It is a pleasure to listen to you, m'sieu. I can promise you I will not be long.'

He hurried away over the creaking and protesting floorboards, banged the counter-flap, and in a matter of seconds the hiss of steam announced that the coffee was being made. The walls vibrated with the strain of his descent into the cellar, and M. Pinaud had hardly begun to smoke a cigarette before he re-appeared, laden with a tray, smiling and triumphant.

'There you are, M'sieu Pinaud. The coffee I am unable to improve—I always do make it strong and scalding hot. The liqueur I hope you may find even better—certainly stronger. It should be—it is six months older. I told you last time it all depends on how long you keep it. I had to go down to the cellar—the bottle on the shelf behind the bar is for the passing motorists.'

M. Pinaud laughed.

'Thank you. Yesterday—driving my car—I might have resented that remark. Now, as a pedestrian and the owner of a smoking wreck in a field, I can appreciate your discrimination.'

The proprietor poured the coffee, filled the wineglass to the brim with liqueur, and left the bottle on the table as he had done before.

M. Pinaud sipped at his glass, at first slowly, and then with increasing speed, feeling the glow and the warmth of that fantastic liqueur spreading and encircling, like some vast, outspread and comforting hand, every part of his inside.

The proprietor had not exaggerated. He was a truthful man. This one was even stronger, if such a thing were possible, than the previous one he still remembered so vividly.

The coffee too, had the same well-remembered effect. Black and scalding hot, it seemed to cause that all-embracing and comforting hand to open out and spread tender, questing and yet potent fingers whose caressing touch combined all their gentle qualities into one vast and assuaging glow . . .

He refilled his glass and drank again. His thoughts were wild and bitter, sad and confused.

He had been badly shaken by the accident and his

narrow escape from a hideous death the day before—far more shocked than he realized—and quite apart from his superficial aches and bruises, there was a definite mental reaction.

Germaine had wanted him to see the doctor at once, but gently and firmly, and with masterly tact, he had conveyed his reluctance to consult a man who was certainly a qualified doctor, but for all he knew might well be a successful murderer as well...

Oh yes, Dr Poidevin might have said, the human body and nervous system does not care for strain and tension. Faltering—tired—depressed? Of course. Only natural. Hardly surprising. Here—take two of these, M'sieu Pinaud, one before and one after each meal. They will soon put you right.

And when he was found dead, and therefore no longer a nuisance with his eternal questions regarding Louise Voisin, there would be generous and heartfelt concern from all the sympathetic people in Vervion.

Poor M. Pinaud—not as young as he was when he brought such fame and glory to the *Sûreté*—terribly shocked and shaken at having to watch his beloved car burn to a wreck—over three hundred thousand kilometres he told me, which sounds incredible—and then the reaction and the depression—the aftermath and the let-down—he always seemed a moody man to me. Oh yes—a charming manner—but quite definitely a moody and introspective type—even suicidal...

And who better qualified to sign an autopsy certificate than Dr. Poidevin, who enjoyed the privilege of being not only local but police doctor as well?

Therefore he had used all his eloquence to its best

effect, and had no difficulty in convincing his beloved and anxious wife that his check-up, which he fully agreed was both advisable and necessary, could just as well be held at the hospital in Locroix the next day, where and when he would have to go to the local offices of his insurance company with regard to the claim for his car.

He drank more coffee and refilled his glass. His thoughts ran on and on.

There was an old saying about an ill-wind. He would have had to pay another large bill to Dufour for repairs to the slipping clutch. That at least had been eliminated. If the farmer Nardin kept to his word—and he looked the type who would—he might not come out of the whole affair too badly. His car was undoubtedly falling to pieces. If he could get a replacement one it would certainly be in better condition.

He felt in his inside pocket, took out an old envelope and a pen, and began to make rapid notes, which he hoped he would be able to read the next day. He had telephoned, on his arrival home, for an insurance claim-form, but in the meantime it would be just as well to jot down some of the numerous and infuriating particulars these gentlemen invariably required.

Time of accident, date, locality, spectators, witnesses and weather conditions. Make, type, model and registration number of car, ditto of other car involved, nearest road-sign, particulars of previous claims etc, etc. Most of this he could note now, while he was thinking of it, and therefore save time when the form arrived.

This was indeed a remarkable liqueur. It not only

warmed body, soul and mind, but it also definitely helped to clarify thought, purpose and concentration. It would be stupid—uncouth—the act of a half-wit—not to take advantage of help so generously offered.

With these sentiments in mind he emptied his glass and immediately refilled it.

He thought then that he would never make a successful salesman, in spite of all the arrogant convictions he had repeated to himself quite recently at this very table in this same *cafe*. His own character seemed to compel him to sympathize and identify himself with the buyer instead of dominating him—or her, as the case might be.

The ultimate—indeed, the only—object of travelling as a salesman was to sell. Every other consideration should therefore naturally be subordinated to this end.

He sighed deeply and reached for his glass.

Then he thought of Louise Voisin. The eager, vital and charming young girl who had called on them to sell her brushes and household appliances. The bruised and decomposing corpse he had found in his woodshed. The girl who had found copulation a joy, a comfort and a pastime.

There was so much to think about. Which one of her lovers had been unable to face the thought of acknowledging the paternity of her child? Who had decided to end it all—swiftly, secretly and permanently? Who had taken his hand-axe and used it on that lovely and intelligent head with as little compunction as he would have split a log of wood?

She had known Robert Macon carnally since they

were at school together. The joys and delights of translating adolescent dreams into physical realities—exciting and unbelievable—happen to each generation with ever recurring and never-failing wonder. Would he have killed the one who made so many of his own dreams come true?

And Dr. Poidevin—had his calm and cool competence acted as a challenge to a mind and body so eager and intense? Had she devoted particular care to demonstrating how two or three index fingers, so sensitive, impersonal and assured in assessing the soreness and the roughness of an infection of the labia, could be so differently and excitingly exercised in stimulating a clitoris?

It could have been like that. He did not know. It did not look as if anyone would ever know . . .

Then there was General Correvon. He was old, but from the look of him, still virile.

His wife, although they had never met, because of her influence and connections with the Minister, would almost certainly have come from a well-born and distinguished upper-class family. High-ranking career officers in the French Army could not afford to marry outside such a circle, whatever popsy they decided to take to bed on Saturday nights. Family and influence were synonymous with a distinguished military career.

She would have been more than strictly brought up, because of her very circumstances and prospects, within the rigid and narrow-minded confines of the previous generation's concepts of right and wrong.

That is to say, she would have been told by a stern and unyielding mother, at an age when such instruction was not only suitable but necessary, that when she eventually made a happy and successful marriage—which was naturally her parents' dearest wish—certain most unpleasant and definitely unhygienic things would inevitably happen to her.

The best advice any mother could give to her daughter was to keep her eyes tightly shut and try to ignore them. There was really no possible way of avoiding them. This—regrettably—happened to be how the male beast was made . . .

But the ineffable bliss and unbelievable joys of children and a family—which, incongruously enough, nature had inexplicably made dependent on these rutting contortions—more than compensated, as every young girl had to find out for herself, for these degrading, shameful, disgusting and distasteful practises . . .

And so, the family—the necessary reason for the marriage—having been created, nursed, fed, cared for and cherished, educated and dispersed, the general would almost certainly have been told very soon that such male bestialities were hardly decent or suitable for people of our age, and may even have been relegated to a separate bedroom in another part of that large and luxurious house. There was enough choice.

In that case, what would the general have thought of Louise Voisin—to whom sex was a joy and a song, a dream and a dance, an inspiration that gave the very meaning to life, or at least—lying on her back with legs widespread—to the sun in the sky, bird-song at twilight and the rustling whisper of leaves in the breeze-beckoned branches above her head . . .

He took more coffee from the fresh pot the proprietor had already brought him and refilled his glass. Then he looked at the level of the liqueur in the bottle in astonishment and disbelief.

Why, with such a unique product, should anyone start putting it into smaller bottles? Surely this was a sign of the niggardly and small-minded pettiness of this day and age, when everything cost more and was usually of inferior quality, so that to give value for money was no longer possible, since money had none, and to give a day's hard and conscientious work in return for fair wages was therefore the exception and not the rule.

He would have to ask the proprietor why and for what reason such a magnificent liqueur should have been put in a smaller bottle.

Having decided this vitally important matter, he returned to his thoughts of Louise Voisin.

There were two more who were suspect. His own employer, Armand Brissac—who had suddenly needed a large sum of money recently. For what purpose?

Had she sat naked in his workroom one night, trying on all those exquisite rings until she found the one she liked, delighted with the skill of this man who had repaired her alarm-clock so that she could use the long and uninterrupted hours of the night to their best advantage?

In that case his own employment would soon cease, and if and when he ever got another car, he would probably have to find something else to sell.

And what about Dufour? Here was a healthy man, a

hard worker, with presumably normal and healthy appetites. If what was available for the asking had been so freely and generously displayed when she got out from her car, as he had recounted, then it would have been abnormal if he had not been interested . . .

And usually the indication of an excessive interest by a wife in her mother was never the sign of a thriving marriage. Wives usually went so often to their mothers to complain of their husbands' shortcomings. This was a pattern as old as history.

He finally got home, not without a certain amount of difficulty, since the pavement, for some inexplicable reason, seemed no longer to bear any relation to the road.

Indeed, it only lasted for a short distance, outside a few of the principal shops, and then disappeared, to be replaced by the lane that led to the church and his home.

It was strange, he reflected, that he had never noticed this pavement before. In any case, no-one ever used it, except mothers with young children. He had always walked in the road. So did everyone else.

Perhaps, therefore, the only strangeness had been in finding himself using it, he thought charitably. And what is more, he castigated himself sternly, you know perfectly well where you are and how to get home. So why are you making such a fuss, Pinaud, about a trifle like a pavement?

Germaine took one swift look at him, removed the latch-key he had left in the lock, and with supreme and wifely tact suggested that it might be a good idea if he went straight to bed.

'There is very often quite a delay between a severe shock and the resultant reaction,' she assured him, with all the love and kindness of her truly Christian nature clearly audible in every word she uttered.

And not only in her voice—there was that same love in her eyes as she looked at him—a love and tolerance and understanding far greater than any of the exasperating and infuriating emotions sometimes engendered by the behaviour and certain characteristics in the complex nature of this remarkable and exhilarating man she had married . . .

'That is why I told you to see the doctor.'

He had laid out the long garden-hose before he left to see Inspector Javel, the rubber clamp at one end in line with the base of the house wall in the side passage, ready to be fitted on to the kitchen tap, its coils neatly arranged and tidily concealed behind the broken water-butt as far as the pressure-nozzle at the other end.

He had planned to use this to flush out the drains on his return. His excavations of the gutters had not improved their efficiency.

But now they would have to wait. Nothing could be done now. He was far too tired.

He smiled, and took her in his arms. Then he kissed her with love, tenderness, admiration and respect.

'I promise you I will see a doctor to-morrow. At the moment I am going to bed. You are quite right. Now you know why I married you.'

If you can only sleep for about ten hours, Pinaud, he

assured himself repeatedly in the bedroom, tearing off his clothes, watching with dismay two buttons fly inexplicably off his shirt and hit the wall, and experiencing a certain amount of difficulty with the legs of his pyjamas—if only you can do that, then indubitably you will feel very much better. Or even eight hours, he compromised as he let his head sink gratefully into the depths of the cool soft pillow, or even—

He was asleep before he had finished reassuring himself.

But none of his prognostications and none of his deductions—although they probably were completely correct—were ever fulfilled.

Germaine, who was an extremely light sleeper, was shaking him wildly by the arm, it seemed to him only two minutes after he had fallen asleep.

'Quick—you must be quick—' she told him with an intense urgency, her voice high-pitched and anxious with fear.

'Wake up—wake up now—the shed is on fire—'

He was out of bed in a matter of seconds, his dressing-gown and slippers on in five more, fully awake and conscious of the danger, his mind clear and alert. Even as he spoke to her, the thought came, incongruous in its comfort, that he must have slept more than a few moments.

'Tell me—'

'I slept in the next room not to disturb you. The crackle and the roar of the flames woke me up—'

'All right. The hose is ready. Get on the 'phone to the Fire Station at Locroix. Don't come outside.'

With the last word he was gone.

It was not humanly possible, she thought fleetingly as he charged out through the open door, for anyone to move so fast, and in the same instant she noticed the disorderly pile of clothing on the floor and the two shirt-buttons on the carpet.

It was not humanly possible—and yet he had asked her hand in marriage, and had loved and cherished her, beyond all understanding, for all the long and happy days that lay, glowing with the comfort and the joy of remembrance, reaching back beneath and beyond the arches of the years . . .

And it was with a soft and tender and happy smile on her lips that she ran, proudly and lightly, downstairs to telephone the Fire Station.

The fire was in the first utility shed opposite the kitchen, in which he kept the garden tools, paint and dustbins, the ladders and wheelbarrow, and all the other things one needed quickly and conveniently in bad weather when living in the country.

Opposite the kitchen door—which meant that the flames, which by now were well alight, had only to leap and reach across the narrow side-passage to blister and ignite the aged wooden beams on the other side . . .

He leapt into action with a complete co-ordination of mind and body. He tore open the back door, jammed the rubber clamp of the hose on to the kitchen tap and turned the water full on. The coils of the hose outside were flung apart and scattered in one gigantic heave, the pressure-nozzle turned hard on, and in an incredibly short time he was directing a powerful jet of water into the heart of the leaping and roaring flames.

For long and anxious moments the issue hung in the balance. But he refused to admit defeat and pressed ever nearer to the flames, in spite of the smell of scorched cloth from his dressing-gown and the searing heat in his face.

The stench of burning petrol was unmistakable. He remembered thankfully that he kept his motor lawn-mower in the far shed at the end of the path, together with its tins of petrol.

This conflagration had been started wilfully, in the same way that the jerking of his ladder, the failure of his steering, and the signal of the rocket to warn the tractor of his arrival at the crest of the hill had all been deliberate. He kept tins of paint in this shed, admittedly, and paint burned well, as everyone knew. But paint never burned with the smell of petrol.

Well within the half-hour, he heard the distant siren of the fire-engine. He dropped the hose and staggered a little as he supported himself against the back wall. He had contained, but not defeated the flames. At least he had prevented them from reaching the house.

Now he ran down the garden path to open the outside iron gate, so that the fire-engine could drive straight in and right up to the back of the house.

Which it did.

A swarming and efficient gang of helmeted and asbestos-clad figures immediately made all his efforts seem like child's play, and the fantastic pressure in their brass-nozzled hose gave him the impression that he had been playing with a trickle of tap-water.

But he had saved, if not much of his shed, at least their lovely house from damage and even destruction.

And then Inspector Javel appeared, immaculate in his pressed and well-fitting suit, looking as though he were seated behind his desk at ten o'clock in the morning and far more respectable than anyone had the right to be attending a fire in the middle of the night.

M. Pinaud glanced down at his scorched and tattered dressing-gown, his reddened and blackened hands, and at what had once been a perfectly good pair of bedroom slippers. A birthday gift from Germaine.

'Ah, Inspector,' he said pointedly, and if his voice held bitterness, sarcasm and even a trace of venom, this is easily forgiven. He had been hardly tried. 'It is good to see that you are still taking some interest in the case of the murder of Louise Voisin.'

The inspector's eyes, as usual, were completely expressionless.

'I am the Inspector of Police in Vervion, M'sieu Pinaud,' he replied quietly, and even with a certain dignity. 'I told you I always patrol the town, to keep myself informed of what is going on. A fire in the middle of the night is obviously my business.'

'Yes,' M. Pinaud agreed, trying hard to keep his voice factual. 'I know that this is—or was—a very old shed, with beams and planks that are all highly inflammable. I admit that I keep tins of paint in it—for that the shed was built—and again everyone knows that paint burns well. But I am sure you will agree that it needed a considerable amount of petrol sprinkled well everywhere to create such a successful fire.'

'Agreed. Obviously. Completely agreed. A case of arson. A case—if you had not been here so conveniently with your garden hose—which apparently someone must have overlooked in the dark—a case of terrifyingly successful arson. A case that ties up conclusively with what you were telling me only this afternoon. Someone here in Vervion is trying very hard to eliminate you, M'sieu Pinaud.'

'He has not yet succeeded.'

'No. It is a clear case of arson. But—again—there is no proof. Who could have noticed anyone, at this time of night, coming down the lane to this house, carrying a tin of petrol almost certainly concealed in a bag, to start a fire? There is no proof. That is the trouble. There has never been any proof.'

Then they all said good-night to each other and M. Pinaud went first to have a bath and then back to his bed.

TWELVE

He had planned to visit Brissac early the following morning. It would be better to arrive before he became busy with people coming into the shop.

He needed a certain amount of information before he could satisfy M. Dupuis' doubts as to the quality of the service he might reasonably expect outside Locroix. And there was the exciting news to relate that M. Latour of the same town would be interested in seeing and buying some more new rings.

But by the time he had finished a long and frustrating conversation on the telephone with the Paris office of his house insurance company, trying to convince a bored and languid female voice, whose owner obviously had other and more vital matters on her mind, that this claim of his for a new shed was surely of sufficient importance to justify him speaking personally to the manager, and when that august personage had finally condescended with great reluctance to listen to him, he realized that his plan, although a good one, was not likely to be implemented.

He eventually took his sample-case and invoice-book and walked quickly to the shop.

Brissac was not there. A bright and cheerful middle-aged lady was sitting on one of the two benches in front of the counter.

'Good-morning to you,' she boomed in a hearty voice. 'M'sieu Brissac will not be very long. He is in the back fitting new cords to my watch.'

'Thank you, Madame.'

Then her casual glance became more interested.

'But whatever happened to you? You must be M'sieu Pinaud—just moved into the old house by the church—right?'

'Right,' he agreed, smiling. He had ointment on his scorched and reddened face, sticking-plaster on some of the worst burns and bandages on his hands and wrists. Germaine had proved swift, efficient and capable. But he would have to hire a car from Dufour that afternoon to get to a doctor in Locroix and have the check-up he had promised her.

'There was a fire in my shed last night,' he continued. 'Did you hear the fire-engine?'

If she did not know, then there was bound to be someone in this place who would tell her everything very shortly. Besides, this was the country, where—unlike the big city—people were friendly and liked to talk to each other.

'No. When I sleep, I sleep. Are you all right? Anyone hurt? Your wife—'

He smiled again and held up his hand.

'No-one hurt, mercifully. No damage to anything except the shed.'

'But how exciting. Tell me all about it—'

The appearance of Brissac from the back of the shop

saved M. Pinaud from having to do this.

'Just imagine—M'sieu Pinaud's shed caught fire last night—did you know?'

Brissac looked across the counter gravely.

'So it would seem,' he said dryly. 'No—I did not know. Here is your watch, Madame Ronsard. Thank you—yes, ten francs. And now if you would excuse me, I have some important business to discuss with M'sieu Pinaud here. I am sure he will tell you all about his fire next time you meet.'

She left with obvious reluctance. M. Pinaud held the door open for her.

'Only the shed?' Brissac asked when she had gone. 'No other damage to the house? I heard the fire-engine go past. From your appearance you must have put it out for them.'

Briefly M. Pinaud told him what happened and was about to discuss M. Dupuis and his service problems when the door opened again and a long-haired young man burst in, holding out in his hand a large, square and very complicated looking steel wrist-watch, which—from the appearance of his patched jeans and darned shirt—had cost him far more than what he spent on clothes over a period of years.

'Good-morning, M'sieu Brissac. You remember the watch I bought from you a few months ago—can you fit me a new glass, please? In a hurry.'

Brissac put a watchmaker's glass to his eye and examined the watch.

'Of course. But not while you wait, Jean,' he told him.

Jean looked crestfallen.

'But it was supposed to be an unbreakable one—'

'I know. It was. But they do fall out sometimes. Changes of temperature. I can fit a new round one while you wait. The correct size just presses in. But the shaped ones have to be cut—and this one very carefully too. It has to clear all these small hands on the subsidiary dials.'

It seemed as if Jean might burst into tears at any moment.

Brissac smiled.

'What time do you stop work, Jean?' he asked.

'Six o'clock.'

'Then I will wait for you. Come in and collect it on your way home. I will cut you one this afternoon.'

'Oh, thank you—thank you very much, M'sieu Brissac.'

He was halfway through the door when Brissac called him back.

'Just a moment, Jean. Your receipt—you must have a receipt.'

He opened the large book on the end of the counter, wrote in it quickly, and then tore out and handed to Jean the perforated section of the half-page with its duplicate number.

'Take great care not to lose it,' he said with an inscrutable face, 'Or else I shall refuse to give you the watch. I must keep my books in order and my records straight.'

'Thank you once again. See you to-night.'

And Jean was out of the shop in a flash.

M. Pinaud decided that it would do the doubting M. Dupuis good to hear of this impressive manifestation of the Brissac service and determined to tell him about it on the next occasion he was in Locroix.

The door opened once more. Again the affairs of M. Dupuis were obliged to wait.

This one was female, tall and thin, with an insipid and vapid countenance, made up of dull, apathetic and heavily blacked eyes, a small, peevish and lip-sticked mouth and an insignificant snub nose.

She was wearing apparently only one shapeless and voluminous blanket-like garment, which appeared to combine all the functions of vest, underclothes, petticoat, jumper, cardigan and skirt at the same time. At the lower end it partially concealed, but did not hide, knee-high boots.

In one hand she carried an alarm-clock.

'Mummy bought it here for me as a birthday present,' she began in a high shrill voice. Mummy apparently had not considered it important to teach her to be polite and say good-morning.

'She said it would wake me up every morning so that I would not be late for work. It goes very well. It has gone since she gave it to me, and what is more, it keeps excellent time. But after the first morning, the alarm has never gone off. It is set for seven o'clock in the morning. I have to get up at seven, so as to be able to eat a good breakfast and have enough time to get to work by nine—there are certain things that should not be hurried you know—'

By this time Brissac had the clock in his hand. He turned it over, held it to his ear, and then gave the mainspring key a few turns.

'It is going now,' he said. 'You have already wound

it—'

'Yes. I told you. I wound it last night. It has been going well since Mummy gave it to me. But the alarm only went off once. That is what I told you.'

Brissac moved his fingers and began to turn the alarm mainspring key. Then he stopped in astonishment.

'But this is completely run down. It has not been wound—'

'I tell you I wind it every night, before I go to bed. How could the clock go and tell the time—which it does—if I did not wind it?'

Brissac sighed profoundly and continued to wind the alarm mainspring as he spoke to her.

'Mademoiselle, on a clock of this type there are always—because there has to be—two mainsprings and two winding keys. One spring drives the timepiece train, the other the alarm mechanism.'

'Oh.'

M. Pinaud, who had been listening with great interest, thought it was very unlikely that she knew or understood what he was talking about.

'Nobody told me that.'

'I can assure you, Mademoiselle, that this fact was fully explained to Madame your mother at the time of the sale. I am the only person selling goods in this shop, and this is something I never fail to do.'

If—M. Pinaud reflected sardonically, as he stood there waiting in a fever of impatience for this moron to leave—if Madame the mother had bequeathed her own intelligence and personality to her daughter, then all this misunderstanding was hardly surprising.

Whatever Brissac had taken the trouble to explain, she would either not have heard it, ignored it, or dismissed it as unimportant.

'There,' announced Brissac triumphantly, having finished his winding. He held the clock out over the counter for her to see.

'The alarm-spring is now fully wound. There is a lever here at the side. If you have already wound the alarm and do not wish it to ring in the morning, you move this lever to the word silent. If you need the alarm, move it across to the other side, which is marked alarm. This button moves the alarm-hand, on this small dial, to whatever time you wish it to ring. It is now ten o'clock. Please watch carefully. I move the alarm-hand to that time—'

The thunderous clanging of the bell, which M. Pinaud considered to be even more effective than the siren on last night's fire-engine, interrupted and drowned Brissac's voice, even though he went on speaking, not without some perfectly justifiable triumph in his voice.

M. Pinaud wondered how much of his explanation she had really understood. Although she smiled vaguely and even clapped her hands at the resonant clangour, he noticed that her eyes were still as dull and apathetic as before, without the slightest gleam of intelligence or understanding.

'Oh—wonderful. That is what it did the first morning I had it—but never again—'

'You must wind the alarm-mainspring, Mademoiselle, to give it the power to ring—'

'What an extraordinary idea. I always thought you

Gone to her Death

wound any clock once and that was it—'

She took the clock back from Brissac and put it in one of the capacious pockets of her voluminous garment.

'Anyway—thank you very much,' she said. 'Do I owe you any money?'

Brissac smiled.

'Of course not. Come back if you have any more trouble.'

'Thank you.'

M. Pinaud opened the door politely for her, but he did not merit another thank you. Mummy had probably warned her about strange men and what they invariably wanted.

'She will be back to-morrow,' he prophesied cheerfully, 'asking you to explain why the alarm will not ring when the lever is on silent. Everything you told her went in one ear and straight out the other. There is no brain between them to absorb it.'

Brissac laughed loudly and heartily.

'The mother was exactly the same. I spent half-an-hour explaining to her exactly how it worked. She said she understood. It was perfectly obvious that she had no idea what I was talking about.'

Then M. Pinaud told him about M. Dupuis and his problems.

Brissac laughed again, this time even louder.

'I would not worry about that one, M'sieu Pinaud, if I were you. These country shops are full of small-minded old women, as you will find out, masquerading as male managers.

I can assure you that I am capable of giving a far

better and quicker service here, as you have just seen this morning, than any wholesale establishment in Paris, with its workshops filled with bloody-minded, quarrelling and jealous workmen and a postal service that ignores the urgent label. If necessary I can close this shop, put a notice on the door, get in my car and deliver anything urgent in Locroix within the hour.'

'I am glad to hear that. I will tell him so. And I am sure I will do business with him. Now I have some good news.'

And he told Brissac about M. Latour and his order.

'He is prepared to buy some more, he told me, but he would like something different in design—'

Brissac held up his hand to interrupt.

'Well, first of all—my sincere congratulations on this invoice, M'sieu Pinaud,' he said. 'You really have made a good start. Now if you do not mind waiting a few moments,' he continued, 'while I go to the back and look through my desk—I think it will be well worthwhile for both of us. When I first started thinking of these rings, I made some sketches of patterns I thought might be saleable. I have never had time to make half of them.'

'That sounds like a very good idea,' M. Pinaud told him. 'Perhaps I could even show him your sketches and from them he can order the ones he likes.'

'That is the way to do it. I shall not be long.'

He disappeared into the back of the shop. M. Pinaud waited by the end of the counter. Idly, with no conscious thought except to pass the time, he opened the repair-book which Brissac had just used.

It was perforated down the middle of each page, and

horizontally into four sections, each one of which could be torn out as a receipt. These and their counterfoils were stamped with the same consecutive number, enabling Brissac to identify each repair.

He turned back the pages of the counterfoils. It was astonishing how many repairs Brissac handled in a week. He turned more pages.

Then suddenly he stopped and bent over the counter to look more closely.

The name was familiar. A gold watch had been brought in here for a new glass on the day after that Sunday on which—all expert opinion seemed to agree—Louise Voisin had been murdered...

He stared at the page with a feverish intensity of concentration that brought on the scintillations of migraine to make the letters and numbers quiver and cavort as if in some mocking and macabre dance.

His mind, with that instantaneous clarity which is the wonder of thought, seemed to race with frenzied remembering.

Then, suddenly, he knew what he had to do.

'Would you look after my case and book, M'sieu Brissac,' he shouted at the open door. 'They are on the counter. I will be back to explain.'

He did not wait for an answer, but went out of the front door at a speed that made even young Jean's recent departure seem like a tranquil dawdle.

He ran all the way home, which fact his chronicler (who is concerned only with the truth) feels justified in emphasizing was an achievement, at his age, not without a certain merit.

Several of the respectable female citizens of Vervion paused in their shopping to eye him with pity and wonder.

'There goes that poor M'sieu Pinaud,' one remarked in a loud and penetrating voice to her two companions. 'It is a sight sad to see. Obviously the man has hallucinations. Hardly surprising. One hears that he drinks. He has been seen in The Seven Sons of Aymon. And not only with a glass in front of him, but the whole bottle on the table. That is a sure sign. Just look at him now—he imagines without a doubt, I am convinced, that his shed is once again on fire.'

'I am sorry for his wife,' said one companion.

'At his age he should have more sense,' pronounced the other sternly, and with the same certainty and conviction. 'His face, as you can see, is as red as a beetroot. Any moment now he will drop down dead with heart-failure.'

A stout and motherly looking figure, with a shrewd and kindly face, joined them from the other side of the road and made her resonant voice carry with astonishing clarity.

'Doctor Poidevin, who although an arrogant young upstart, is nevertheless, they tell me, a very fine and capable doctor, has continually maintained that there comes a certain age—not necessarily the same for each person—when all strenuous and violent physical exertion should definitely cease. It is a pity that he does not seem to have voiced his opinions to this M'sieu Pinaud.

'But then all Parisians, it is a well-known fact, are completely mad. All day they rush about in exactly the same way. I feel positively ill myself each time I return from the city.

'Come—come with me, Gabrielle. It is clearly our duty as good neighbours—his wife is really a most charming person and a regular and devoted church-goer—and also a matter of plain Christian charity, for us to walk up now to Doctor Poidevin and warn him what is surely going to happen.'

M. Pinaud neither saw nor heard any of them. He would not have stopped if he had.

He ran around his house to the back. Germaine was at the far end of the garden, on her knees with a trowel in her hand. He could imagine the happy and contented expression on her tranquil countenance.

He waved to her but did not stop.

The upper door of the woodshed was open to enable the logs to dry in the fine weather. He burst in and came to a panting halt.

He remembered the cardboard box, into which he had poured the heap of miscellaneous junk found at the bottom of the wooden packing-case he had broken up for firewood. The box was still there, just as he had left it. He lifted it up on to a tall log and stirred around inside with his forefinger and thumb until he found what he wanted.

It did not take long, and he was still breathing hard, shallowly and rapidly, as a result of his exertions, as he came out again, one hand tightly clenched in his pocket, waved to the patient kneeling figure by the last flower-bed, and walked back quickly the way he had come.

'Inspector Javel—is he in?'

The burly policeman at the front desk eyed him without enthusiasm.

'Have you made an appointment, M'sieu Pinaud? He is a busy man—'

By the time he had finished M. Pinaud was half-way up the stairs.

'He will see me,' he called out over his shoulder, and raced on towards the door of the first-floor office without waiting for an answer.

He did not knock, but burst open the door swiftly and savagely, stepped inside and closed it firmly behind his back. And then he waited there, without stepping forward from the threshold.

For a long moment—across the intervening space that separated them, M. Pinaud in the doorway and Inspector Javel seated at his desk—the two men stared at each other in complete silence.

It was a stillness that seemed to grow and expand and deepen in intensity with each slow second's passing, and all the time it was as if the tension grew and swelled underneath it, palpable, almost unbearable, seeking and yet not daring to rise to break it . . .

It was the moment of truth, which each man could read in the other's eyes.

Then M. Pinaud walked, slowly and deliberately, across the room to the desk.

'Inspector Javel—may I look at your wrist-watch?'

His voice was quiet and without inflection. In silence the inspector stretched out his left arm. The expensive gold cuff-links drew back to reveal the slim gold rectangular watch on his wrist.

M. Pinaud withdrew the hand from his pocket and dropped the small strip of celluloid he had been holding there on the desk in front of him.

'In my woodshed there were two packing-cases side by side. The body of Louise Voisin was in one of them. Can you explain how the original glass from that watch was found in the other?'

He did not wait for his question to be answered, but continued to speak still in that same quiet and expressionless voice.

'With the strain of lifting and heaving the weight of an inanimate body, the muscles of the forearm and wrist swell and expand under that pressure. If a wristwatch is worn under these circumstances, the watchstrap tightens to put on an extra strain which often distorts a shaped case, causing the bezel holding the glass to expand under the pull of the strap and loosen. The glass therefore falls out. The pressure to hold it in is no longer there.

'I have no doubt that if we ask Brissac to compare, he will find that this piece here is the original glass he replaced in your watch on the day after her murder. Shall we both walk together over to his shop, and ask him to try?'

To him, it seemed that the words were pouring out from his lips in a chaotic and frenzied torrent—trying vainly to keep pace with the lightning-like rapidity of his thoughts—white-hot and accusing.

To the man who was listening, tense and motionless, they were cold, calm and factual, awesome in their implication, unassailable in their truth and menacing in their meaning . . .

He finished speaking, and the long moments seemed to stretch out between them, sundering them, isolating them, dooming them to remain eternally apart.

Still the inspector did not reply. Only now in his eyes, in which M. Pinaud had been unable to read any emotion, expression or feeling ever since they had met, there was now torment. There was agony. And there was shame . . .

Which was not surprising, he thought swiftly. The shock and the incredible surprise of finding out the truth had obscured the logical sequence of its inevitability.

Dufour was a highly skilled mechanic. If with his experience he maintained that a split-pin could corrode, rust and fall off, then he was almost certainly correct.

And although the odds were unlikely that both failures on Nardin's tractor had occurred simultaneously, every farmer and mechanic knew that the hydraulics on a tractor, even the best, could be tricky things. And Nardin had impressed him as an honest man who spoke the truth.

Small boys too, have been known to buy or even steal rockets for the sheer undiluted bliss of letting them off in a deserted and lonely place, not only for the ecstatic joy of contemplation, but also to avoid answering awkward questions from interfering parents as to how they came to acquire them.

And last but not least—who would ever have noticed that an Inspector of Police—on his continual, accepted and even meritorious patrols of a small provincial town—wore crêpe soled boots on one occasion?

There would never have been any vestige of suspicion. His presence anywhere, in his official capacity, would have automatically provided a logical justification—even carrying a bag concealing a tin of petrol under his arm, late at night, on his way to M. Pinaud's tool-shed, in which he had reason to suspect that someone had deliberately started a fire—even entering M. Pinaud's woodshed on Sunday morning to check for fire risks and to wait for Louise Voisin's arrival in answer to his invitation to meet him there. She would have been interested to see what the builders had done to the old place she had known since childhood for the new owners from Paris . . .

With the grace and speed of a jungle animal, Inspector Javel was on his feet.

M. Pinaud tensed. The reaching of this man's arm across the desk had revealed the shoulder-holster he wore. M. Pinaud was unarmed. He owned several revolvers, but they were under the bed in an old suitcase. Who ever heard of a detective walking armed around a country town after he had retired?

He tensed with the danger his own vivid imagination had created—that sense of dread engendered by so many years of near encounter with death.

But needlessly, his rational thinking told him the next moment. So many horrors in his life, the fruits of his own imaginative conjectures, had never even happened to him.

How would Inspector Javel be able to explain a dead body with a bullet hole in it, lying inside his own office? The dead body of an unarmed man. He would have to find some other solution to his problem.

An ambitious inspector could have had no use for blackmail, that was obvious. And the higher ranks of the *Sûreté Nationale* do not take kindly to such complications involving their employees.

His dreams and aspirations would have been driving him on, to be awarded a larger and more prosperous town as promotion once he could have claimed Vervion as a model of his tenancy.

'Would you excuse me, M'sieu Pinaud?'

The words were quiet and sad, and hopeless with the acceptance of the ultimate finality.

'Of course.'

He stood aside, with understanding and compassion softening and ennobling the stern hard lines of his features, and waited patiently—enduring and trying to ignore the rigidity of his tension—until he heard the flat harsh report of the single shot.

First of all he felt only an overwhelming sense of sadness at the waste, the pity and the futility of it all. The words of the English poet John Donne came unbidden to his mind:
> Any man's death diminishes me

as vividly and as clearly as if they were being spoken to him aloud.

Then, as the slow minutes passed and he still stood there, alone with the turmoil and the complexity of his thoughts, a tranquil sense of peace and feeling of profound relief seemed to flow into his mind with the great and comforting surge of some giant wave.

Now—for the first time since his retirement—his

prospects seemed more assured. Now—after all the anxieties, frustrations, worries and fears of the past few days—it seemed for the first time that he had a future to which he could look forward with confidence, trust and hope.

Brissac would go on making him those magnificent rings. With the help of M. Latour, Madame Rougement, and some of his other and better clients, he should be able to earn a decent living.

Whatever type of car he got from the insurance company, Dufour—a mechanic and not a murderer—would be fully capable of keeping it running reliably on the road.

Brissac was innocent. Dufour was innocent.

And as and when he would surely desire to celebrate these momentous actualities—why go to spend his microscopic pension at The Seven Sons of Aymon? The proprietor, granted, was a good type, who earned his profit fairly and honestly and well.

But up the hill outside Vervion was the farm of Jules Nardin, a fine and splendid character who not only had saved his life but who also distilled that remarkable liqueur. And even if he sold some of it he obviously kept the best and the strongest for himself. He remembered that he had an open invitation to go up to the farm and sample what was lying not only on the shelves but around the floors of the cellars, whenever he wished.

And there was General Correvon, who apparently was not accepting that lucrative appointment abroad his wife had laboured so assiduously to procure for him. He would be able to call at that magnificent house whenever he felt like a neighbourly visit, and reminisce over the old days in the Maquis—with a little help from that exquisite brandy poured into tumbler-sized glasses.

Nardin was innocent. General Correvon was innocent. And so were Robert Macon and Dr. Poidevin.

It was an exhilarating thought, that now he could enter the establishment of Macon and Son and buy some shirts, which he badly needed, and even ask for a discount if he bought enough.

And an even more splendidly comforting one, that if he went to the surgery as a patient, as Germaine had been entreating him to do ever since he got up, he could rely on some soothing and healing ointment—and not some filthy irritant poison—being applied to all his painful burns . . .

Now he could go back to his woodshed, where it had all begun.

Now he could work, hour after hour, cutting and breaking twigs for kindling, sawing branches, chopping and splitting logs, and arranging and stacking everything neatly and tidily into collective piles, brushing and sweeping the floor and collecting the sawdust and chips for the bonfire at the far end of the garden—and making his woodshed into a model of what it ought to be . . .